Date: 2/8/19

LP MYS ESTLEMAN
Estleman, Loren D.,
Black and white ball

BLACK AND WHITE BALL

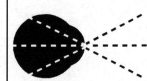

This Large Print Book carries the
Seal of Approval of N.A.V.H.

AN AMOS WALKER NOVEL

BLACK AND WHITE BALL

LOREN D. ESTLEMAN

THORNDIKE PRESS
A part of Gale, a Cengage Company

GALE
A Cengage Company

Farmington Hills, Mich • San Francisco • New York • Waterville, Maine
Meriden, Conn • Mason, Ohio • Chicago

LIBRARY OF CONGRESS CIP DATA ON FILE.
CATALOGUING IN PUBLICATION FOR THIS BOOK
IS AVAILABLE FROM THE LIBRARY OF CONGRESS

ISBN-13: 978-1-4328-5780-6 (hardcover)

Published in 2018 by arrangement with Macmillan Publishing Group, LLC/Tor/Forge

Printed in Mexico
2 3 4 5 6 7 22 21 20 19 18

To Ian Smith,
in his memory;
and to
Barbara Smith.
Neither ocean nor pale
can part true friends.

Gray is the new black.

— Anonymous

Me

ONE

Canadian Customs has a reputation for courtesy and gracious behavior, particularly toward visitors from the States. You can look it up somewhere, probably. I've never seen it in practice.

The one I got this time had the lean, lupine face, ginger-colored eyebrows, and pale blue eyes of the born bully. He stared holes through my ID and threw it back through the driver's side window. I caught it between my knees.

"What's your reason for visiting Canada?"

I said it was business. I knew if I said pleasure I'd be pulled over and my seats torn apart.

He let me go, possibly because the car behind me was flying a Red Wings pennant from its antenna. That was good for a cavity search.

Maybe things are different at other crossings. With an entire foreign country sprawled just three minutes from our city by bridge or tunnel, expatriation is just a matter of commuting to work. Detroiters are an invasive species.

Things improved two hours later when I pulled up in front of the Cabot Inn in Toronto. It was a bed-and-breakfast with its name in cursive on a sign swung from chains and a lot of spires and gimcrack; some moldering lumber baron's idea of a castle on the Rhine. I'd just yanked the parking brake when a cream-and-blue Le-Baron turned in front of me into the little parking lot and the driver got out, hitched up his relaxed-fit jeans, and came around to open the passenger's door for a pneumatic blonde in a sundress printed with penguins for some reason. She carried a shopping bag.

His disguise was as convincing as Groucho glasses. Some men can get away with a NASCAR sweatshirt and *Duck Dynasty* ballcap, but Guy Lennert looked like a man who wore pinstripes on his pajamas. Also the dumb cluck was driving a company vehicle.

The brass at Fiat-Chrysler didn't care about that or the blonde, only the six hundred thousand dollars he'd managed to skim off investors' dividends. He'd spent the last three years rounding down their checks and pocketing the odd change before sending them on. The thing was so simple there was no telling how long it might have continued, but then he'd failed to show up for work three days in a row, and when someone called his home his wife said he'd told her the company had sent him to the Paris Auto Show. That was when the CFO took a closer look at the books.

I had no more business working for any of the Big Three than Lennert had wearing a beret on the Champs-Élysées. They have their own security, whose payroll could support the CIA, FBI, NSA, and Campfire Girls. I'd taken on the job as a favor to the wife he'd left behind. The interview had gone this way:

"Amos. You've kept your hair."

"Had to," I said. "It goes with my gray suit. You haven't changed."

"God, I hope you're just being kind. I earned every sag and wrinkle."

"Is it Mrs. Lennert now, or are you a modern woman?"

"It is and I am; but it'll be McBride again soon. Do you still drink?"

"Old friends keep asking me that. Every-one seems to think I had a reason to quit."

Karen left me standing in a living room that opened onto the rest of the ground floor in every direction and went into the kitchen to clink, rattle, and pour. The house was in Farmington Hills. It wasn't the biggest in the neighborhood, but the smallest would have swallowed my three rooms and garage like the last fish to the right in a food chain chart. Christmas was coming, and she'd livened up the neutral tones with red candles in green holders and a light glowing in a glass on the mantel with a cardinal painted on it, but the corner where a tree might have stood belonged instead to a torchiere lamp with an amber shade. I remembered she had a phobia about keeping flora indoors. I remembered a lot of things about her from long ago.

She came in carrying two tall glasses on a tray. Today almost any woman can be beautiful given the options, but a truly handsome one is a matter of genetics. She'd retained her slim athletic build under an off-white linen lounging outfit, and if anyone had colluded in her auburn highlights, she'd made the right hire. A frothy pale-green scarf hung loosely around her neck, which is usually the first thing to go, but her high cheekbones and golden-brown eyes drew attention away from it to her face.

14

Even the tiny lines around the eyes were more interesting than distracting; you expected them, like the craquelure in a Renaissance painting, and would have been disappointed if anything had been done to fill them in.

"Scotch, as I recall." She set the tray down on a slab of black volcanic rock. "Didn't you always say people don't change?"

"Could be. It sounds like me." I let her sit down in a leather sling chair before taking a spot on a gray love seat. We clinked glasses and sat back. I asked if she was still a nurse.

"I retired when Guy got his last promotion. If he's spent all he stole on that blonde, I may have to go back for a refresher course. Things change fast in medicine."

She'd told me most of it over the phone. I said, "You're sure it was him with the blonde. They set those surveillance cameras too high at the border. You see the top of a lot of heads — if they're accommodating enough to lean out the car window."

"The man I spoke to at Chrysler said the guard pulled them over and made them get out. Guy probably made a joke. He thinks he's witty."

"He must have wired the money somewhere if they let him go. They'd have found that much cash in bulk. They're more thorough letting people in than out."

"I wouldn't be so sure. He can be clever when he makes the effort. It took a call from someone in the State Department to make them give up the tape. The search went that direction when I found recent travel brochures of Canada in Guy's sock drawer."

"Two governments are on the job, three if you count Fiat-Chrysler. You don't need me, Karen. I work out of a shoebox with hand tools."

"Somehow I doubt the Dominion will sweat bullets looking for a man who brought money *into* the country. The U.S. marshals are working on a tip they boarded a private plane in Newfoundland and are on their way to Europe by way of Greenland. The company's put all its offices there on alert."

"Tips pan out sometimes."

"I don't buy it. Guy and I flew in a puddle-jumper just once; he dragged me off at the first stop. He's terrified of flying in anything smaller than a seven-forty-seven. But you know the system. Nothing Little Wifie has to say carries any ballast."

"So divorce him for infidelity."

"I don't give two snaps about the other woman. She'll find out soon enough the sables and silk aren't worth the freight."

"Desertion, then."

"Not just yet. Before he left he cleaned out our joint account so it would look like he was traveling on his own dime. I want him found, prosecuted, and convicted so I can bring civil action against him. I deposited my life's savings when I got out of scrubs." She started to drink, then glared at me over the top of her glass. "What are you grinning at?"

"We just got into my wheelhouse. If it weren't for people wanting to get even, I'd be retired myself."

"Same old Amos. I remember now why we're not together anymore." She drank. "Any regrets?"

"Only the time I wasted on the ones I had."

I got what I needed from her and we finished our drinks. At the door I said, "I'm sorry. About Guy."

"I'm sorry about more than that." When she smiled, the laugh lines radiated. "When you find him . . ."

"I'll call you first. Last time the feds put me on hold, I spent twenty minutes listening to Dionne Warwick."

So here I was, planning my assault on the Cabot Inn and listening to a CBC talk show host griping about government health care.

I'd have thought I was back home except for the way he mispronounced words like "sorry" and "schedule."

The coin fell on the side of Pickett's Charge. I got out, followed a flagstone walk to a front porch with a rocking chair on one end and a wood-burning heater on the other, and went through a door with a card in it that said I was welcome. A shallow foyer contained the usual rag rug, potted plant, and open staircase leading to the second floor; also a smell of cinnamon strong enough to stop a runaway freight. This was coming from a little gift shop that had probably been a side parlor under British rule, stocked with soaps, candles, T-shirts, and glass paperweights that showered glitter-dust on miniature Torontos.

A fat ledger rested on an oak podium next to a bell. I slapped the bell. A woman came out the gift shop door and stopped with her hands folded at her waist. She looked to be the same vintage as the house, with hair as fine and white as refined sugar caught up with combs and a black woolen dress that cried out for white lace but hadn't any. She had flesh-colored buttons in both ears and more lenses in her spectacles than they have on Mount Wilson.

"A man and a woman came in a few

minutes ago," I said. "What room are they in?"

"Do you want a room?" she yelled.

I had to repeat myself, exaggerating the consonants. She stared at my lips, moving hers in mirror-image.

"Are you with them?"

I cringed. She had only the one volume. "I told them I couldn't make it. I'd like to surprise them." I folded a ten-spot and held it between my first and second fingers. She toddled forward, adjusting her glasses, not slowing as she came close. I wondered if I should get out of her way. Finally she stopped with her nose almost touching Alexander Hamilton's.

"You're American?"

"Guilty."

"I knew it already. Americans think they can buy anything."

She was looking up at me now, with cloudy eyes and a face set like reinforced concrete. I put away the money and got out my ID folder with the honorary Wayne County sheriff's star pinned to it, held it two inches in front of her face.

"You're not a policeman."

"Not guilty of that. I'm working for the man's wife."

"What's she need a private enquiry agent

for? She's upstairs with him."

"Not unless he's a Mormon." I slipped the photo Karen had given me from the pocket of the folder, the most recent she had of Guy Lennert. It was a full-length shot someone had taken of the couple in front of the Blue Heron restaurant in Bloomfield Hills. Both were in tailored suits, his black, hers hunter green, pressed close with arms entwined.

"This isn't Mrs. Linden."

"Right again. It's Mrs. Guy Lennert. If he signed your register with any other name, some graphologist will work it out."

Water rushed somewhere in the building. Someone was taking a shower.

"I can't —"

She stopped. Even she'd heard it, coming from upstairs. It wasn't the pipes banging.

Two

"What room are they in?"

"Really, I —"

But I already had the big book open on the podium. The last page I flipped to was only half-filled with signatures. "Mr. and Mrs. George Linden" were registered in 203. I hit the stairs running.

Waste of energy. Two-oh-three was locked, and from the look of the paneled oak door and brass lock I'd have had to go back down to the first floor for a running start. The shoulder I used for battering was more brittle than it used to be. I called down to the landlady, and my scream must have been persuasive, because it took her only five minutes to climb twelve steps. I kept my ear to the door the whole time, but it was as soundproof as it was un-bust-down-able.

She had a *Downton Abbey* chatelaine fastened to her waist, supporting a bronze ring the size of a softball on the end of a retractable chain with ten keys dangling from it. Of course it took her another minute to find the right one, holding the ring half an inch in front of her goggles, but when she got to it with a little huff of victory, I snatched it out of her hand, ring and all. The chain caught and I almost pulled her down onto her face.

A dead bolt shot back into its socket and I slung the door wide, banging it into the wall and reaching from reflex for a gun I knew wasn't there. Embezzlers usually don't put up that kind of fight.

Someone thought different. That smell never failed to throw me back to my first day on the army firing range: the brimstone stench of sulfur and burnt powder.

I pushed the door in Aunt Gertie's face — a more chivalrous act than it sounds — and turned the knob that shot the bolt home. The nearest thing to a weapon nearest me was a chubby brass lamp on a pedestal table under the wall switch. I yanked it off the table, snapping the cord at the plug with a fireworks show of sparks, and swung it up by the neck. It looked quaint trailing its frilly pink shade, but a bludgeon is a bludgeon.

And another waste of time I also didn't

have as much of as I used to. The bird had flown. That much I got from the open double-hung window across the room from me, the tatted pink curtains shimmering in the wind from Hudson Bay; or wherever the wind comes from in that part of the world.

Just for kicks I crossed to the window — it was open a few inches, letting in outside chill — and looked out on a residential neighborhood no different from the ones I was used to, not counting Detroit's West Side, where the pedestrians wear Kevlar to visit the corner market. The old man in the fedora walking a dustmop terrier might have been a fleeing murderer in disguise, but he waited too patiently for the dog to take a leak against a bus stop bench to attract my interest. The rose trellis decorating that side of the house was tailor-made for Romeo and Raskolnikov alike to gain access to the room and egress from it. It was made of iron, not flimsy lath.

Which left me holding a faux-Edwardian lamp, staring at a corpse on the floor and a naked woman shrieking for the police.

Not my best visit to our friendly neighbor to the north; but then again, not my worst.

The detective's name was Weber. I'd been hoping for something hyphenated, or maybe

Gallic; I knew a genuine Mountie would be too much to ask for, but a little cultural color seemed like a reasonable request. He shook my hand and said that if he could call me Amos I should call him Bert.

"Not Albert?"

"We're not so formal as you Yanks might think."

He showed a fine set of uppers behind a fair moustache. Both went well against his tan. I hadn't expected to see one that close to the Arctic Ocean, or for that matter good teeth; but the Old Dominion boasts a first-class dental plan. He might have been thirty or fifty in gray wool worsted, cut by a man who'd apprenticed in diamonds. His head was entirely bald, some by nature, the rest by way of a razor. It glistened like wax fruit.

"Fire away, Bert."

"I might start with your relationship to this fellow at our feet."

Strictly speaking, he wasn't at our feet; I sensed a poetic turn in the Toronto cop's approach to the worst in crimes. Guy Lennert lay off to the right, on the edge of the fleece rug in the center of the room, fully dressed except for his shoes, both legs stretched out toward a Queen Anne bed poofed up with quilts, pillows, and padded cylinders, and his fair-haired head jammed into a corner. His brow wore a Kali-style tattoo in the form of a bluish hole square between the eyes. The eyes themselves were felt circles, like furniture pads. At this stage they were good for nothing else.

"Here." Weber handed me a fold of white linen from an inside breast pocket.

I wiped dried blood from my right cheek. "Mrs. Linden" — now sequestered in a vacant room, so that her story might or might not check out with mine — had gotten her licks in before I'd wrestled her into position long enough for the landlady to call the authorities. The handkerchief came away as pink as the curtains and lampshade. "I can put the cleaning on the expense account."

"I'll put it on mine." He accepted its return. "You ought to have those scratches looked at. Human germs are more virulent than animals'. I wonder why that is?"

"Animals don't kill for money."

"What makes you think that's why Mr. Linden — Lennert, according to you — was killed?"

"Pass, Lieutenant. Or is it *Left*enant? I don't speak the language."

"Inspector. Meaningless, really, except for a couple of hundred more loonies in the bank. I'm still performing the duties I was as a sergeant." He folded his arms, frowning down at the dead man. "Between us, you're probably right; though my chief won't enjoy the prospect of one of your American hired killers invading our country. We give you hockey players, Tim Horton's Donuts, Michael J. Fox, and this is what you offer us in return."

"You also offer us yards of snow from Alberta, coins we can't spend, and bad coffee. You're American, too, don't forget. So far no one's dug a channel across the continent."

He laughed, without the ring of irony. I started to like him; I didn't like that. "I haven't the science at my command, but experience tells me this man was slain with a thirty-eight — using your country's measurements — or a nine-millimeter — using ours and on occasion yours. Mrs. Lennert, and for now we'll pay her the courtesy of addressing her by that name, says she was in the shower and didn't hear the shot. Do you agree with this account of the circumstances?"

"I never argue with a naked woman."

"Are we sure it was a professional killing?"

"I wouldn't sign a statement saying it, but it was too clean for the average civilian. No footprints, no spent shell casing, which means he probably used a revolver."

"He had time to pick one up that was ejected from a semi-automatic."

"He might have, if he thought it wouldn't bounce or roll somewhere out of sight so he'd have to get down on his hands and knees and search. But if he did, it still means he was cool enough to leave the place as he found it, not counting the cadaver."

"Pros often ditch the weapon at the scene. It would be untraceable if he's as good as you say."

"He couldn't be sure he won't need it if the getaway's messy. He caught a break when he heard the shower running on his way in over the sill and found Lennert alone in the room, but he couldn't be sure she wouldn't come out before he left. Another thing these boys seldom leave behind is a witness."

"Maybe it wasn't a boy."

"I wouldn't rule it out, but hit women aren't as common as you see in the movies. The mob trains most of them, and it isn't an equal opportunity employer."

"So now the Mafia has come to Canada. Your country is building its wall on the wrong border."

I played with a cigarette, not intending to light it. The local forensics team wouldn't thank me for giving them one more clue to subtract. "Not enough outrage, Inspector. Try again. The silk shirts have had a presence here since Prohibition. Unless Lennert had something doing in that direction, I don't like them for this. This button might have studied under them, but right now he's got more enemies in the boardroom."

"There's always your client."

"I thought of her first, but I told her I doubted he had the money with him." I didn't add I'd checked while the landlady was comforting the blonde outside. Lennert had a few hundred on him. They hadn't unpacked, so the drawers were empty, and the suitcases didn't have false bottoms. The bathroom was small enough to frisk in a couple of minutes. The woman's shopping bag held lingerie only. The shams, pillows, spreads, and bolsters on the bed kept me busy long enough for my cheek to stop bleeding. It was like strip-searching Marie Antoinette. I put it all back together just in time to greet the inspector.

"Still," he said, "hell hath no fury."

"It hath in her case. Anyway, why hire me to look for her husband if she had someone else doing just that, with the bonus of taking him out when he found him?"

"Finding people is your specialty. Maybe

you were the Judas goat and didn't know it."

"I don't like to brag, but I know when I'm being followed. As often as I've been, I look for it out of habit."

"A corporate contract, then. Or have I been reading too much John Grisham?"

"Fiat-Chrysler wouldn't hardly stoop to throw the switch for less than a couple of hundred million. If this were my case, I'd take a look at the investors who got fleeced the most. On top of the best motive, they're in the bracket that can afford to hire an expert. You get what you pay for, and if you're the type that haggles, you stand a good chance of dealing with an undercover cop."

"Can I take you at your word it's *not* your case?"

"You can dip it in bronze and hang it in your office. When it comes to hunting contract killers I'm so far out of my league I can't see the scoreboard."

He was still holding my credentials. He looked at them again. "For a private detective, you seem to know a lot about the trade in murder."

"I know a little bit about a lot of things."

Car doors slammed below. That would be the morgue wagon and the boys and girls who collect butts and blood spatters. Weber gave back my folder. "Wait downstairs. We need a statement you *will* sign, and I'll arrange an escort to see you don't catch any red lights between here and the bridge. Or do you prefer the tunnel?"

"I haven't made up my mind yet. The day I'm having, I could fall off one or drown in the other."

THREE

"If you had your choice of any time in history to live, which would you choose?"

"You got that from a book," I said. "Carson McCullers."

"I didn't say it was original to me."

I frowned at my uninvited guest. Leo Dorfman was the lawyer people had in mind when they told lawyer jokes. He'd made himself a millionaire several times representing the kind of client the no-nukes said would be the last creatures to survive the apocalypse: cockroaches, corrupt politicians, hit-and-run drivers, serial rapists, pedophiles, stars of reality TV.

Professional killers.

Which were my personal grudge.

We're all of us potential murderers, but pulling the trigger on a perfect stranger for a paycheck is worse than strangling women who remind you of your mother. At least there's a personal element there.

31

This was no new prejudice, but it was fresh again since Toronto. That story was three weeks old and had dropped off the wire for lack of a lead.

"Humor me." He slid his checker — black, always black — to the last rank on the board and snapped his fingers until I crowned him. He traveled with his own board and men: I don't think there's a way to rig the game, but if there is, he'd know how. "At my age I'm still a student of human behavior."

Just what age that was depended on the observer. Some people are thirty forever, but for reasons known only to him, Dorfman had stalled at eighty. He'd go on being eighty until he crumbled to dust. His face was unwrinkled, but the skin had shrink-sealed itself to bone and his hair was the color and texture of fishline, combed sideways across pink scalp. Although he was retired from daily practice, he put on a different three-piece suit every day, with a black silk knitted tie on a white button-down shirt; permanently in fashion, a stopped clock like the rest of him.

"I'm partial to the roaring twenties," I said, blocking his next move. "My father was always talking about how much fun Prohibition was."

"It's overrated." And with that I added another twenty years to my estimate of the time he'd spent on earth. "You took your life in your hands every time you drank, and the drys were worse than Hari Krishna, clustered on every corner shaking their fingers in your face."

"Okay, you pick one."

He jumped the man I'd just moved. "Here. Now."

"Should I be flattered?"

"No. I'm a lawyer, don't forget. Until you can prove to me in court that it's possible to travel through time, I've got no choice but to be here, now. So I don't dwell on it."

"Then why bring it up?"

"I needed a subject for conversation. You won't work for me, so I was running dry."

"You know why I won't."

Everyone's entitled to legal representation, but Dorfman had a reputation for performing as a buffer between hit men and their potential clients. A dozen investigations had failed to produce any evidence, so I hadn't thrown him out yet; but nor would I take any job he offered.

"You're pretty picky for a man in your tax bracket."

I slid a checker onto a square, but kept my finger on it. "Remind me again why these visits. I ran an errand for you once, but that was before you pled the Fifth twenty-six times in front of a grand jury. It was so long ago I forget what it was."

"I doubt that. When Cecil Fish was the prosecutor in Iroquois Heights I came to you with a tip that he was planning to frame Joe Minuto by sneaking a rock of heroin into his coat at a wedding. You had Joe's tailor sew up all his pockets."

"Not original to me. Frank Costello did it first."

"I knew Frank. I never heard that story. He was the most close-mouthed man I ever knew; and I haven't exactly traveled among the garrulous and gregarious."

"They're like moths. Born without mouth parts." I stretched and yawned; but he never took hints. I looked at my watch. "I'm interviewing a client in Birmingham in an hour."

"You haven't had a client there since Steve Jobs was in diapers. You think I only come here to play checkers?"

I'd been wondering when he'd come around to it. His mind wasn't on the game or he'd have cleaned me out ten minutes ago. I made a bonehead move just to clear the board.

"A client of mine is getting a divorce," he

said, skipping over my pieces straight to the corner and scooping up the loot with the same hand.

"I don't touch divorce. Neither do you."

"I recommended a good gal. You want to leave your wife with nothing but her girdle, you want a broad to represent you. They go after their own like wolverines. It's the wife he's worried about, and that's where you come in."

"He wants the girdle too?"

"You better ask him. I don't want to be disbarred for telling tales out of school this late in the game. I'd rather they earn it."

"I won't work for you, Leo. You said it yourself."

"It wouldn't be for me. This is a favor I'm doing him. Fish had a solid case against him once and I broke it over my knee. After that I had to beat the clients away with a stick."

"What's his name?"

He looked up from under the white awning of his brows. "If I tell you, you'll turn down the job."

"O.J. back in trouble already?"

"That amateur?"

He told me the name, but it meant nothing to me, and he wouldn't be drawn out. I didn't try; a trio of congressional committees had dashed themselves against that rock. After he folded his board and left, I called Detroit Police Headquarters. A broken windpipe came on the line.

I said, "Lieutenant Stonesmith, please."

"If you're reporting a missing person, she's no longer with that detail."

"I'm not. I heard she was back in Major Crimes."

"She was the first appointment when they reinstated it under the new chief. You reporting a crime?"

"Maybe. I need an expert who can tell me whether it's major."

Wind whistled through the pipe. "You don't call this number when you want to tell jokes, mister. Believe me, you don't."

"I believe you. Lieutenant Stonesmith, please."

The phone clicked. I waited for the dial tone; but he hadn't hung up, just put me on hold. It clicked again and a voice came on that sounded like honey boiled in Kentucky bourbon.

"Stonesmith."

"Amos Walker, Deb. Get tired of chasing runaways and restless wives?"

"Not really, but I knew who to put back on staff, and the chief was desperate. I got a guy in the FBI. He lets me know who's

36

under investigation. Want a job?"

"Sounds like it's not just the chief who's desperate."

"Our evidence room moves more merchandise than Costco, my best officer from the old days beat a suspect into jelly, and since cops turned into silhouette targets out on the highways and byways of this great land of ours the training course is emptier than Kmart. When I file my reports, *I* file my reports. They can't even dig me up a clerk. Am I desperate?"

"You don't want me, Deb. The last time I was in uniform I punched my way out of it in the locker room, and I was a lot less hot-tempered then."

"Well, let me know if you find anyone dumb enough to take the oath. What's the squeal today?"

"I need everything you've got on a guy named Peter Macklin."

The silence on her end broke in half when a chair squeaked and a door clicked shut.

"All right, what's the job?"

"There isn't one yet. That's what I'm trying to find out."

"Unless I don't know you the way I think I do, there isn't one."

"Now I'm curious. What have you got on him?"

"Not a damn thing, that's the problem. Come down here. This is better in person."

FOUR

The only thing feminine about Deborah Stonesmith's office was a spray of flowers on her desk, and it wasn't for looks. The scent battled the fetid stench of rot from inside the walls.

Thirteen Hundred Beaubien, the traditional home of the Detroit Police Department since 1922, had been in a state of near-condemnation for most of the century, a victim of municipal looting from the mayor's office all the way down to pest control. The upper floors were an uninhabitable mix of asbestos, black mold, and rats the size of toy poodles. Homicide had fled to the old Third Precinct, leaving the ancient pile to assorted felonies — some of which included homicide.

The flowers fell short of the mark. They put me in mind of a funeral service I'd attended many years ago, in a place thousands of miles away, in a musty tent.

Stonesmith had a private life, but you wouldn't know it to look around the place where she worked. The walls were blank, the nasty government green making a bilious haze through several coats of taupe. No snapshots, no plucky cat posters, not even the obligatory academy class photograph. Nuns kept gaudier quarters.

Her desk was orderly, stacked with urgent papers closest to hand, less pressing files next to it, and a steel mesh wastebasket for the rest. It would be cleared by quitting and new stacks waiting for her in the morning.

She caught me looking. "I'm a file clerk, not a cop. I keep a record of hits-and-runs, drive-bys, and bloody domestic dustups to pass along to the chief so he can say violent crimes are down — not counting murder. We had sixteen last weekend, and that's not this year's record."

"How do you stand it?"

"I call in sick those days captains' bars are handed out. It's one step too close to the top when the voters turn the rascals out of office. I got a kid in medical school and another starting kindergarten."

She didn't look old enough even for the toddler. The lieutenant was a tall trim-sailed woman with a cinnamon-toast complexion, brown eyes clear as planets, and a profile cadged off the tomb of an Egyptian queen. She liked big hair, hoops in her ears, and dusky-rose business suits with skirts.

I sat facing the desk and accepted the coffee she shoved my way in a blue-and-gold DPD mug — the kind they sell for souvenirs in the lobby. I'd swiped a couple in interrogation. She brewed it herself, in a Bunn with her name Dymo-labeled on it, so it actually tasted like something that came from a bean. "I got steered to this client," I said. "Leo Dorfman at the wheel."

"Shit. Is he still alive? Of course he is. I get a brimstone whiff whenever the gates of hell swing open. I haven't had one since Castro kicked."

"You wonder why they bother to put up gates. What's it say on Macklin's sheet?"

"Hasn't got one, apart from questioning; which happened maybe once, before I made the CID. Most of the time Dorfman was already here when Macklin showed. Showed," she repeated. "I reviewed the file after you called. He's a virgin as far as bracelets are concerned. Turned himself in whenever he found out we were looking for him, for Man One or better."

"When did perps start making better citizens than everyone else?"

"About the time we started putting cops

on *Candid Camera* instead of the bad guys. I'd tag him tomorrow if I had a print, even a partial. DNA's too much to wish for."

"Serial?"

"Serial killers I can feel for. They're like a natural disaster, no one's fault except maybe rotten parenting. A man who'd cap someone he didn't know just to make rent is worse than an animal. They only kill to survive. I'd trade half my pension to clock him on just one stiff. It would clear the books on a couple of dozen."

"The mob?"

"Where do they all get their start? But he went indy a long time ago."

"Risky. It isn't just the aggrieved party who runs the chance of hooking up with an undercover cop."

"He covers the spread. He presents his bill before getting into specifics: Everything you own."

"Who's that desperate?"

"People who are unlikely to undergo a change of heart and holler cop. He has them bring in their income tax forms going back three years, bank statements, investment portfolios if any, the equity on their mortgage. Then he takes half up front, in cash. This is all snitch stuff, hearsay. A jury can't buy it, but any cop can, on the faith of his gut."

I rolled the mug between my palms. "How does he know the bills aren't marked, or their serial numbers recorded?"

"I've worked that angle, too, but I haven't been able to track down his laundry service. On his terms, he could clear a nickel on the dollar and still make out."

"Weapon of choice?"

"So far it doesn't look like he uses poison."

"Now you're pulling my leg."

"How do you think he's lasted this long? By the time we sort through the gunmen, garroters, and skullbenders and decide it isn't a specialist, the case is as cold as Jimmy Hoffa's dick. When it's bullets he does lean toward revolvers. They don't jam as often as a semi-auto and don't leave shell casings behind. Not that he carries the piece more than a couple of blocks, but it slows us down."

"Stab in the dark. Thirty-eight?"

"Uh-huh. I was wondering when you were going to get around to Toronto, but it's slim. That's their baby unless and until something breaks over here. We got the report on the old man you spotted outside the window. He didn't see anything. He says. We don't hold the monopoly on noninvolvement, or murder for hire, despite what you read in their brochures."

"Shame on you. Hands across the border and all that."

"They're too picky for my taste. They won't extradite to capital-punishment states. Lifer place like ours, they'd probably insist we feed them gluten-free."

"Got a picture, or is he like Dracula?"

"I pulled it after you called." She opened a drawer and skidded a glossy sheet my way. It was a driver's license photo and vitals downloaded from the computer files in Lansing. I'd seen that same receding hairline, nondescript nose, and bland expression on three faces that week. He was a few years younger than I was. Height 5'11", weight 170, eyes gray. They say the eyes are the windows of the soul. His curtains were drawn.

I gave it back. "That's the closest thing to a walking brown paper bag I've ever seen."

"His best asset. The eyewitnesses he left breathing gave us swell descriptions, if you like stick figures."

"Dorfman says he's going through a divorce."

She nodded. "Laurie. Half his age and smarter than any moll you ever met. Had her down here a couple of times, comparing

44

our exes. She knows more about mine now than I do about hers. She's either more afraid of him than she is of us or she stands to clean up by not sending him over to the system."

I grinned. "Seriously, 'moll'? Someone's been watching TCM."

"A girl's got to unwind. I read where Napoleon took his mind off war by playing chess."

"I read where he cheated."

"Another thing we have in common."

I drank coffee. She made it strong without making it bitter. You have to be born knowing how. "You painted her in broad strokes. You're a better judge of character than that."

"That's like telling an artist he can draw a straight line. It's in the job description." She shook her head, making the hoops wobble. "I can't decide whether she took it into the marriage or learned on the run. She cracks about as easy as bedrock, but to talk to her you'd think you'd tapped the debutante's ball. That's if you can find her. We couldn't justify spending the money to keep her under surveillance, but the last spot check we made, she'd sold her place in Southfield and didn't leave a forwarding." The hoops stopped moving. "Tell me that isn't the job, Amos: fingering her for the thirty-eight-caliber divorce."

"Come on, Deb."

She wouldn't come on, though. Her eyes were as dead as asteroids.

I said, "Okay, so past performance doesn't guarantee future results. If he's as slick as you say, he doesn't need me to flush her out. Anyway Dorfman gave me a contact number, and if he's got it, so has his client."

"What is it?"

"You know better than to ask."

"If there's one thing I do know, it's to ask anyway. Amos, if she knows where Macklin is, we might nail him before he can ditch any evidence that would put him out of our misery for years."

"Yours; not mine. Not sharing that kind of information is what puts the 'private' in private detective. It's all I've got to offer that you can't."

"We could sweat it out of you at County."

"I wish you'd try. You can't buy advertising like that."

"You're taking the job?"

"I won't know that until I know what the job is."

She looked down into her cup, reading the grounds. "You don't tell me how to be a cop, I don't tell you how to be a snoop."

"Sounds like you're telling me anyway."

The phone on her desk rang. She rested a hand on the receiver. "Just watch your step. Whatever Macklin's up to, it's to his neck."

Thirteen Hundred is as easy to get out of as it is to get into, which is not at all. I think the city reverses the direction of all the one-way streets on a rotating basis. If you don't concentrate, you wind up driving a pile of scrap. I'd negotiated three of the four when I realized I'd taken on a passenger.

"Keep driving. Don't run any lights."

I spun the wheel, taking aim at the lamp-post on the corner.

But the man on the right side of the backseat, out of range of the rearview mirror, had learned the same lesson I had. I was climbing the curb when something cold and hard crackled the hairs on the nape of my neck. The air was dry that day; a steel muzzle generates enough static electricity to light a room. I swung the car left, not quite in time to avoid skinning paint off the right fender, but with enough space between me and the driver of the panel truck behind to hit me with his horn instead of his bumper. I drove, with a gun at my head.

■ ■ ■ ■

HIM

■ ■ ■ ■

FIVE

It's difficult to acquire a gun in Canada: The government in Ottawa practically spelled it out on its license plates.

Like so many civic mottoes, it lied.

The country was a hunter's paradise. The demand far outweighed the legal restrictions. You just had to know a guy who knew a guy, and not so well either.

The guy Macklin knew directed him to four blocks of business district off the Queen's Highway and a shaggy dog of a shop elbowed in between a Rexall Drugs and a butchery with a take-a-number dispenser visible through the glass door and no takers. The shop he needed was paneled in knotty pine. There were racks of camo suits, deer whistles in baskets, pinup queens on retro tin signs, packages of beef jerky, and dead flies embalmed on hanging strips that looked like curls of whittled wood. The head of a moth-pocked moose looked down

51

on the counter from high on a wall with a brown Christmas wreath drooping from one antler. It wasn't this year's wreath. It was too far out of reach to bother retrieving.

The place had a stale cedar smell that might have been piped in — bootlegged, like the pine and taxidermy, for the benefit of Yank tourists who thought the world had stopped turning north of Lake Erie; in that particular location there were no cedar trees, only birch and jack pine, stunted and twisted like arthritic old men. A computerized cash register was the only thing in the shop that hadn't been smuggled in from Jack London, and it wore a deerskin hairside out. The man behind the counter had on leather suspenders and a red-and-blackchecked shirt buttoned to the throat. It was too hot for flannel with the radiator going full blast; sweat drops glittered on his bald head and the rash around his neck generated heat at a distance of ten paces. He looked up from whatever he was doing when the front door opened, disturbing sleigh bells attached to a harness.

Macklin stopped at the counter. "Gullstrand."

"You just missed him. He's been dead eight years."

"They said in Windsor it was seven."

"*Who* said?" Baldy had returned his concentration to his project. It involved a precision screwdriver and some unidentifiable metal parts scattered on the counter.

"Doesn't matter. It's nearer six. Gullstrand sold me a thirty-eight on a forty-five frame six and a half years ago and he wasn't a ghost."

"You Peters?"

Macklin nodded.

The bald man's hands were thick-veined and mottled, but they moved so fast the fingers were a blur. In three seconds he had the parts assembled and Macklin looked into the muzzle of a two-shot over-and-under .22 magnum pistol.

The face on the public side of the counter remained bland. They were the kind of features even the man in Windsor wouldn't remember enough to describe them in a way that would do anyone any good. Baldy registered disappointment at the lack of surprise on the customer's face. Macklin stood motionless while Baldy disassembled the piece as swiftly as he'd put it together. He spread his palms on the counter. "Still got that remounted thirty-eight?"

"I lost it."

"Too bad. I'd've bought it back for more than you paid. You always so careless?"

"Always."

"Wait here."

"I go with you."

The counterman looked again at that expressionless face, nodded, and flipped up the gate at his elbow.

Macklin waited while he drew out a key on an extender attached to his belt and unlocked a steel door with a painted woodgrain behind the counter. A sign bolted to it read OWNER DOES NOT KEEP CASH ON PREMISES. When the man opened it and held it for him, he inclined his head forward. The man went in first.

A windowless storeroom took up most of the ground-floor space. It smelled of disinfectant, dust, and the vanilla odor of gun oil. An exit door, steel also but lacking cosmetic paint, was chained and padlocked, contrary to the fire laws, and a surveillance camera mounted high on an electric swivel prowled the room with its unblinking red eye. Gray steel utility shelves stood perpendicular to the walls, with aisles between, lit by fluorescent tubes that flickered and buzzed when the wall switches were palmed up. The shelves contained folded flannel shirts, heavy-duty dungarees, more camo, ear-flapped caps, insulated boots, vials of doe urine, and other items that were on display in the shop. Here as there, no sign of firearms was visible.

A number of yellow-painted steel drums sporting HazMat warnings formed a row against the back wall. The bald man lifted the top off one, releasing an earthy smell and a glimpse of cut-up carrots nearly filling it to the top.

"Deer feed," he explained, plunging both arms to the elbows in the pile. "Draws water like a shop vac. You could store a car in here for five years and it'll come out clean of rust like it never left the floor. Cars keep getting smaller, you'll be able to do just that in a couple-three years. Your Washington and its fucking EPA."

Macklin said nothing, which was the extent of his store of small talk. The man rummaged, stopped, spread his feet, and lifted out a transparent forty-gallon trash bag, grunting under the weight. Inside were handguns, rifles, assault weapons, and un-attached sniper scopes, all sealed in thick semi-opaque plastic. "I got M-sixteens, Mac-tens, Uzis, a reconditioned Kalashni-kov: You name it. Claymores, if you care to relive the good old days in 'Nam. Had me a cherry Tommy, but I sold that to a Capone buff last month." He separated two feet of camo-painted steel and plastic with two grips and a barrel as big around as a plastic toilet tube and held it up. "Grenade launcher. Take out a platoon of Isis ragheads with one squeeze of the trigger."

"Let's see that Rossi."

Baldy took out a blue revolver with a four-inch barrel and lowered the sack to the floor. He pulled open the seal with a ripping sound, slid out the weapon, a .38 with a four-inch barrel, freed the cylinder, and ran it up and down his opposite arm, making it buzz, like in a western. "Sure you don't want a semi-auto?"

"Yeah."

He grinned. " 'Get rid of that revolver. They're always empty when you need them most.' Jimmy said that in *Kiss Tomorrow Goodbye*. Cagney?"

Macklin held out his hand.

The man surrendered the gun. It had a checked walnut grip, warm to the touch and a little worn. Macklin inspected the empty chambers, extended it at arm's length at shoulder height, aiming at the wall, and squeezed the trigger. The hammer cocked and struck the firing pin with a sharp snap. He spun the revolver, offering it back butt-first.

"Stiff. Let's see the Smitty."

The bald man resealed the Rossi in its

package, laid it on a convenient shelf, and dug another blue .38 revolver out of the bag.

It was a Bodyguard Airweight, hammerless, with a two-inch barrel. This time he handed it over without demonstrating the cylinder action. The butt was Neoprene, still shiny from the manufacturer. It smelled like a new toy. Again Macklin inspected the chambers, aimed at the wall, and worked the trigger. The Smith & Wesson responded smoothly, bringing forth the same crisp snap.

"Where can I try it out?"

From between two stacks of shelves the other dragged a square fiberboard carton filled with dirt. "Floor sweepings," he said. "I get all the use out of stuff everyone else throws out; just like Henry Ford."

"How about I knock ten percent off the price every time you spin a story?"

"Hey, it's a slow day." But the bald man shut his trap.

He stepped to another shelf stacked with shallow boxes labeled THERMO-SURE UNDERWEAR, counted down from the top, slid one out, and lifted off the top. He drew out a box of cartridges and carried it to his customer. Macklin took one, blew on it, inserted it in a chamber, adjusted the cylinder. He pointed the barrel at the carton on the floor. "Noise?"

Baldy pounded his fist against the nearest wall. "Lath-and-plaster. Stuffed with asbestos. Don't tell the inspectors."

The side of the carton was stenciled CANADIAN CLUB. As Macklin took aim, the bald proprietor stuck his fingers in his ears.

The report rang off the walls. Macklin lowered the weapon and looked at the ragged hole the bullet had torn through the triangular space in the first A.

"History?"

"None to speak of. Service station robbery in Saskatoon last April. It wasn't fired."

"It will be once more if you're telling another stretcher."

A pair of palms shining with callus came up. "I bought this place at Gullstrand's estate sale, month after he croaked. After all this time, I made that kind of blunder, I'd've hosted my own. Ask Windsor."

"I did. That's why I'm here. How much?"

"American?" When Macklin nodded: "Two grand even. My business, I don't got to charge tax." He tried a grin; couldn't manage it.

"Quote me another price."

"I can't beat Bass Pro, you want to go that route. I'm thinking you don't."

Macklin gave him points for showing

spine. "Fifteen hundred."

"I got to make some profit!"

"You will, if that service station heist isn't a dodge. You paid more than three hundred, you'd've been out of business before I got here."

"Seventeen and I'll throw in the box of ammo."

"Six."

"Six *boxes*? Hey, man, I was just kidding about the ragheads. I sell ordnance, I don't ask questions, but if you're fixing to go into a church or someplace, make a donation in lead —"

"Six cartridges." Macklin plucked the spent shell from the cylinder and held it out.

"Fifteen hundred." Baldy put the shell in his pocket. He waited for the cash to change hands before he tipped six fresh cartridges into the customer's palm.

Macklin opened the door to go out, but turned to glance back through the gap as the bald man tugged the top off another yellow drum and stuffed the wad of bills into a sea of green.

OWNER DOES NOT KEEP CASH ON PREMISES, the sign said. He hoped for the owner's sake he was more truthful than his advertising.

SIX

The car was what they used to call a mace; Macklin was too long away from the people he once associated with to keep up on the terminology. Anyway it was a code the cops could crack, often with the cooperation of the crooks who used it.

Which was one of a host of reasons he'd dropped out of the underworld and gone solo. The colleague you confided in could have a dozen killings on his sheet and still put himself in good with the law by whispering in the correct ear.

Maybe it had always been that way. For all Macklin knew, the myth of the code of silence was a cop's idea, made up to lull the guilty into spilling their guts to each other.

Call it what you like, the car was a ten-year-old Chevrolet Impala with a week-old title, antedated and distressed to show wear in the creases and present the right shade of yellow. The VIN agreed with the number engraved where the original had been filed away from the block and smeared with grease that matched the rest of the engine. Stolen in Wisconsin too long ago to interest the insurance company, it had the pedigree of a mongrel, and the color of the chalky finish was best described as sun tea filtered through bad kidneys, but the tires, brakes, and transmission were new and heavy-duty shocks installed, courtesy of a warehouse filled with unused Soviet military equipment in Kiev. With just enough rust and mud and missing a wheel cover, it was as nearly invisible as the man who drove it.

The environmental equipment, of course, was false, rigged to fool emissions tests during random stops, but doing nothing to hinder the performance. The man who'd sold it to him in Chatham said he'd bought the design from Volkswagen a week before it got in trouble. "Turns a dog of a four-cylinder into a sixty-six Mustang. Breaks my heart to let it go, tell you the truth. You bring it back in good shape, I'll buy it back six bits on the dollar. You won't get a deal like that in the States."

He wouldn't be selling it back. He'd lined up a speculator to scrap it when he was finished with it and sell it to whoever got the bid to build another bridge between

Detroit and Canada.

The performance was likely as advertised, but he wasn't impressed. High-speed chases were for cowboys. The low profile and under-the-radar history were more important to him, along with simple reliability. In his work, the real successes died in their beds without leaving a mark.

There'd been a delay — which he'd allowed for — while he waited for U.S. plates. If he was pulled over for any reason with a Canadian registration, his American license might make the authorities suspicious enough to trace it to its forger, and to determine that "Max Peters" had died at the age of two the year Macklin was born, and therefore could not have a valid Social Security Card in his name. The plates were from Nebraska, a break: The state carried no associations to most of the rest of the world. Contestants on *Jeopardy* routinely did not ring in when the subject came up.

It was a thin tightrope, he had to remind himself; this constant quest for invisibility. After a point, it attracted attention by its very obscurity. Personal camouflage was a must. He routinely traveled with a canceled ticket to a baseball game involving a contender for the most recent World Series in his wallet along with the obligatory ancient condom, a souvenir ballcap suitably crumpled between seats, and a few travel brochures picked up at Visitors Centers along the way: historical exhibits, natural features, and such. Of course, this required some knowledge — not too technical — of the subjects involved, or at least an expression of interest. One side of his brain must be reserved for this, keeping the other side locked in on the target his client had paid him to eliminate.

He drove on provincial roads and surface streets, always at the speed limit or just under, making only fueling stops and using restrooms where he didn't have to ask for a key. He was hungry, having skipped breakfast, but he didn't stop to eat. There'd be time enough for that when the job was behind him. When he worked, he preferred to keep the flow of blood to his brain instead of his digestive system. It was mid-afternoon of a gray December day when he entered Toronto and made his way to the residential section.

There was no reason to notice the car parked in front of the Cabot Inn, except that it was unnoticeable, much like his own: a forty-year-old Oldsmobile Cutlass, blue and battered, with decades of grime turning the vinyl top, white originally, the color of spoiled custard. He cruised past without turning his head, but the corner of his eye snagged an impression of a well-built man past middle age climbing out of the driver's seat, wearing a suit and topcoat as unforgettable as the vehicle. The overcast hung low enough to show that the car's dome light didn't come on when the door opened.

Which might have meant anything from neglect to a short-circuit; but Macklin's own first act after obtaining the Impala was to take its dome light out of service.

He found a spot around the corner and came back on foot, giving the man time to enter the bed-and-breakfast. He wore the Airweight in a belt clip under his fleece-lined leather coat. The Cutlass' tires were in good shape, the exhaust pipe showing no rust under a skin of dust. The driver's door was locked; likely so was the passenger's. Not an insurmountable problem, but getting around it might draw the attention of neighbors. He strolled on past and around the next corner, noting the plate number on the way.

The man was a non-civilian, if not precisely law. Macklin's senses told him that. Cut and run? No. Just do the job and get out. Forget the frills; they were never strictly part of the deal. Keep your weight on the balls of your feet in case the alert sounded.

He turned a corner yet again, putting himself behind the inn. The antique iron trellis he expected was in place, and from its appearance almost as good as an exterior staircase. The roses that had scaled it in spring and summer were now brown-stemmed and brittle. He gripped it with both hands and tugged. It was secured to the building, the lath struts sound.

He'd seen floor plans and photographs of the building inside and out, thanks to the website maintained by the local tourist facilities: It was a nationally registered historic structure built by a nineteenth-century lumber magnate who'd destroyed all his competition and driven away his wife and daughters, then turned philanthropic as he'd neared his Maker. Most useful were the pictures taken recently, enabling Macklin to locate all the guest rooms. His scout was a deliveryman with a legitimate service, bringing a package addressed to a tenant who'd moved out a few days before. While the old woman who managed the house was looking for a forwarding address, he'd found the most recent entry in the guestbook on a podium, reading "Mr. and Mrs. George Linden," the name Guy Lennert and his female companion were using in Canada.

They were in room 203. Only one of the four windows on the second floor was lit, and it was the right one. With only Lennert's Chrysler in the parking lot, apart from a Toyota with Ontario plates belonging to the old lady, the likelihood of anyone else staying there that time of year was slim.

You could wait to be absolutely certain; but that time never came. You had to supply your own certainty, and be prepared to correct the situation in a split second if you failed.

The thorns were the only immediate danger — a snag could slow you down or leave evidence behind in the form of torn cloth or broken skin, both loaded with DNA — but with the blooms shriveled, he could see and avoid them, memorizing where they were because he'd be moving faster when he came down. Climbing didn't come as easily to him as in years past, but he kept in shape and got to the second floor without breathing heavily.

Someone had opened the window three inches, possibly to let steam out. He could hear a shower gushing, but the door that muffled the noise wasn't airtight; the glass was slightly clouded. He listened, heard no sounds of movement. He peered through the gap above the sill, braced to clamber down if he were spotted; a peeping Tom rap he could beat, even a weapons charge, if he couldn't get rid of the revolver or run fast enough.

There'd be no running yet. Lennert, looking like all his photographs in spite of his casual dress, was alone in the bedroom in his stocking feet, combing his hair in front of a mirror attached to a dresser. If Macklin had the conscience of a normal man, he'd have been comforted by the thought that the man's last thought was making himself look good for his lady friend when she came out of the bathroom. There was a superstition even in his profession that a victim slain in terror would be waiting for revenge on the other side.

He wasn't superstitious, and for that matter the thought didn't occur to him. To his point of view, Lennert was dead already.

Something — possibly a faint creak caused by his weight on the trellis or a premonition — distracted Lennert from his reflection. He was turning toward the window, holding his comb like a gun, when Macklin rested the barrel of the Airweight on the sill at a slight angle and shot him in the forehead.

There was no need for a second shot for safety. The wound was square in the center and the way he fell said it all: turning a little on one foot the way a tree twists away from the last blow of the axe and tipping plank-stiff off his heels. Macklin was halfway down the trellis, moving quickly but remembering where the thorns were, before the body struck the floor.

He leapt the last three feet, bending his knees to absorb the impact, but instead of running took off at an easy lope, like a man not wanting to miss a crossing light. The revolver was still in his hand, but in the slash pocket of his jacket, out of sight yet handy if needed to clear a path. He paid attention to his peripherals for potential eyewitnesses. You couldn't expect to eliminate a bevy of them in an open situation, but Leo Dorfman built a better defense when he knew how many to expect during Discovery; a legal process Macklin had yet to face in a long career.

He'd cased the neighborhood long-distance, identifying it as working-class, with most of the residents employed during the day; barring the odd sick-out, the risk was minimal, and it looked as if he'd caught a break. At least he saw no movement in windows.

He slowed down as he approached an old man guiding his Yorkie toward the base of a bench belonging to a bus stop, but the man's back was toward him, and the padding of feet in the grass alongside the sidewalk didn't turn him.

Whether the man heard the remote scream that followed, Macklin never knew. By then he was around the corner and climbing into the Impala. He started the motor and pulled gently away from the curb into a street empty of traffic. At the next corner he turned left and glanced up at the rearview mirror. The abused-looking Cutlass was parked in the same place, still minus its driver.

He dismantled the Airweight and stopped at several scenic lookouts — deserted when he visited — along Highway 401 to dump the components into Lake Ontario. After that he delivered the Impala to the scrapyard in London, then walked eight blocks and hailed the first of a succession of cabs, never riding far enough to attract the drivers' curiosity. The last, in Sarnia, took him across the Blue Water Bridge into Port Huron, Michigan, during evening rush hour. The U.S. Customs officer compared the driver's and passenger's faces with their license photos and waved them through.

SEVEN

Macklin was living in Warren pending the outcome of the divorce, sub-letting a condominium from a retired General Motors engineer currently wintering in Key Biscayne. The décor and furnishings wouldn't have been to his taste even if he cared about those things: heavy on distressed dark wood, brushed brass, and windows with slats intended to make them look mullioned, but which kept falling out, startling him into defense mode. He'd considered removing them, but that would mean a visit from a representative of the condo board, which upheld uniformity of window treatments. In his case, avoiding attention was work-related, not paranoia. He missed owning his home.

Ornamental details meant little. The issue was shelter, not style. The location was close enough to the sprawling GM Tech Center to hear the experimental models roaring around the test track; an annoyance to many, but to him a convenience when conducting a telephone conversation he didn't want his neighbors to overhear.

Like this one:

"You owe a commander in Lansing a C-note," Leo Dorfman said.

"Is it worth it?" Macklin asked.

"I'd call it a bargain at his rank."

"I could get the same information from a sergeant."

"Lieutenants and worse have to sign in when they run a plate, and report the source of the request. Seriously, you're dickering?"

"Why start now? Give me what you got."

"It's a small world. I hired Cutlass guy once."

"What's a lawyer doing driving a car twice the age of my son?"

"Not a lawyer, a private cop, and a good one. Amos Walker. Spelled the way it sounds."

"About six feet, one-eighty, brown hair going gray?"

"Not so gray when I used him, but now, probably. He's a neighbor, lives and works in Detroit. His thing's missing persons."

"What was he doing in Toronto?"

"Ask him."

"Why should I expose myself?"

"Because I said he's good; and good's what you need considering your situation."

Macklin listened to a driver changing gears at ninety. "You're the one with the in. Sound him out. Use that checkerboard of yours."

Ironically — or perhaps not so, based on his observation of human nature — the less legitimate and socially acceptable of Macklin's two occupations was the one still in demand.

He'd spent years building up a retail camera business, run by others in his employ who knew nothing of his outside interests, whose profits had allowed him to declare a reasonable amount of income on his taxes. In the years of his apprenticeship with organized crime, he'd seen too many bright lights extinguished for overlooking Washington's curiosity regarding lavish expenditures on little or no reported income. They languished in prison, condemned not for felonies innumerable, but for stealing from the government.

Macklin had learned from their example. He'd never concealed a dime of profit from sales, deducted no more (and no less) than what was allowed for expenses, and in twenty years his returns had gone unquestioned, enabling him to stash the money he made outside the system and to live off it comfortably but not extravagantly, without calling attention to himself.

When photography went digital, he'd made the conversion (deducting the cost from taxes), and lost customers of his developing service, which was the largest part of the profits. He'd stayed in the black mostly through sales to professional photographers, who wanted the best equipment and were prepared to lay out for it. Then along came cell-phone cameras. Never mind that they couldn't compete in quality with the lowest-end Canon or Nikon: Your average customer will choose convenience over performance a hundred times out of a hundred. Polaroid had proven that. He'd sold out at the first blip in the market, losing a bundle but not as much as competitors who'd held out longer hoping against hope, and put his broker to work finding medium-risk investments for what he'd managed to make away with. He wasn't as concerned with financial security as with the loss of his placid front. Too much federal interest in how he supported himself after his legitimate business went under must inevitably lead to local interest in the details. A five-year jolt for tax evasion was one thing, life for Murder One something else.

Professional killing was a horse of another color, in terms of the commercial market; another species, in fact. The faster the march of technology gobbled up trade that had existed for centuries, the more John and Jane Doe found reasons to eliminate each other the analog, non-digital way.

He was paid in cash: Small bills naturally, worn, the serial numbers non-sequential. Any marks not detectable by the naked eye would be rendered worthless by way of his laundering system into the Third World, where black lights were still science fiction. Half up front — fifty percent of the client's net worth — and the rest on proof of completion. He deposited getaway stakes in several banks under different names, each with corresponding identification, and each deposit well under the ten thousand dollars that financial institutions were required to report to Washington. If one cover was blown, he had the others, and if all were blown, he had cash stashed in several secure venues, with the rest wired by computer to numbered accounts in Andorra, the Cayman Islands, and Switzerland.

The total was substantial, although hardly in *Fortune 500* territory — if there were such a popular index for clandestine income.

Which was comforting, especially in view of the message that had come his way by blind email, along with photos he'd never seen before of Laurie, his estranged wife, sniffing a tomato at the Eastern Market (a hangout for them both in better times), swishing down a mall corridor in a sundress and oversize sunglasses, hair bleached nearly white in the summer sun; strolling a familiar street looking flushed, healthy, and heartbreakingly young in a jacket and billed cap designed for fall weather; sipping a steaming drink in an oversize mug gripped in both hands, looking out a frosted window in a heavy winter sweater. The images were arranged sequentially by season, the last doubtlessly captured since the first heavy snow the first week of this month. They were unposed, and likely she hadn't known they were being taken.

He read again the terse message that accompanied it.

Dorfman had summed it up when he'd said "your situation."

Macklin closed the file, then typed in Amos Walker's name.

Even the internet struggled to find him. The man appeared to have no website, no

Facebook page — no presence, in fact, in twenty-first-century terms. The only proof he existed were his licenses allowing him to drive and conduct investigations, his name in newspaper files, and an old record of petty arrests, mostly for withholding information in open police cases — one instance serious enough to have led to a temporary revocation of his professional license — but no convictions.

A face that had been lived in, but not to the point of serious wear, solemn but with something in the eyes (hazel, said the official description) that looked like trouble, much of it for the wearer. Broad streaks of gray, but he'd kept his hair, and from what Macklin had seen of him in front of the Cabot Inn he hadn't fudged when filling in the height and weight blanks: No indication of flabby living, he was prepared to accept that much based on his brief observation of the man in person; although he thought he'd seen the signs of an old injury when he'd climbed out of his car.

Macklin brought his email back up alongside Walker's picture and read again the message his anonymous correspondent had sent with the photos of Laurie:

$100,000 CASH.

JUST BECAUSE SHE DOESN'T WANT
TO LIVE WITH YOU DOESN'T MEAN
YOU DON'T WANT HER TO LIVE. MORE
SOON.

It was a sum he could manage without
paupering himself; whoever was behind the
message would be aware of that, and that
few in Macklin's position would risk expo-
sure by balking.

Whoever was behind it was wrong.

Walker was still looking at him, as if he'd
read the words and was waiting for Macklin's decision and whether it would involve
him. The answer to both questions was easy.

EIGHT

Macklin's own unreported income could fit inside one of the zeroes in Leo Dorfman's, but if anything the lawyer lived even more modestly than his client, in a one-thousand-square-foot house in Redford Township, built during the 1970s and never renovated: the orange shag carpeting and avocado kitchen appliances had survived obsolescence and were probably on their way back into style. An artificial pink-tinted Christmas tree preened in the dining room bay window, sparkling with tinsel and aglow with fat red-and-green electric bulbs on the old-fashioned kind of string that went dark whenever one burned out.

"Lyla's idea," Dorfman said, inclining his white head toward his wife of fifty-three years, hanging exterior lights on the firs planted outside the window, her nose as red as Rudolph's. Her coat trimmed with faux fur and black knitted watchcap belonged in the pages of *The Bag Lady's Home Companion.* "I'd remind her we're Jewish, but I just don't have the heart."

It would be news to many that he had one of any kind. There wasn't a cop in metropolitan Detroit who didn't call him a "criminal attorney" without an involuntary twist of the mouth.

The counselor's only personal concession to the season had been to add a gay sweater vest to one of his funereal suits. Of the two, Apple Annie with her credit account at Neiman Marcus and the undertaker with cardinals embroidered on his chest, the visitor couldn't determine which was the more incongruous.

But then *undertaker* was too conservative a description for Leo Zephaniah Dorfman. His FBI file associated him with more burials than the Ebola virus. The reports were worded carefully, *alleged* prominent in every paragraph. He'd never been convicted of conspiracy to commit murder, or even placed under arrest for suspicion. Unlike Macklin's, his personal transactions were all legitimate and spelled out on his Form 1040, investments based on payments for his legal services. A score of intensive investigations had failed to turn up even one client who'd arranged a professional killing through him. The clients, of course, weren't talking, and the billing hours, expenses, and consultation fees reported in the lawyer's books could all be traced to legitimate advice. The fact that he hadn't set foot in a courtroom or filed a brief in more than a decade did not constitute evidence.

They took seats opposite each other at the round oak table where the old man — in semi-retirement now — conducted business. It was in the room with the bay window, so the quarters were cramped, shared temporarily with the grotesque tree, which smelled more strongly of pine than the genuine article, thanks to regular attention by way of an aerosol can. It reminded Macklin of an old car whose rearview mirror was hung with evergreen-shaped artificial fresheners; and of a childhood he didn't care to remember.

Dorfman lifted a liter and a half of Captain Morgan's along with his eyebrows — disconcertingly black, despite the crisp snowdrift of his hair — and when his guest shook his head, filled one of a pair of cut-crystal glasses nearly to the top and tinted it with a dollop of eggnog from a cardboard carton. He stirred the mixture with a little finger, sucked it clean, and cupped the glass between his palms, searching the contents for tea leaves and the fortunes they told.

"He's clean, Walker is. I copped a look at the checkbook in his desk when he went to the can. I carry around more cash in my wallet."

"You carry around more cash than anyone I've ever met. And there's another book that tells a different story. I shouldn't have to tell *you* that."

"He took a few calls while we were playing checkers. Turned down an advance of ten thousand from a husband who wanted to know why his wife took two hours coming home from a job fifteen minutes away three times a week. It was legit. I recognized the name."

"He could've taken the call anytime when you weren't there. The fact that you *were* reeks."

"Wait till I finish. While I was studying the board he made out a check for the rent on the office. I can read upside down; anyone can, in my line. It left him with a dollar-ten in the bank."

"He's a private cop. Lawyers are his turkey-and-trimmings. He knows you can read upside down, backward, and under water, same as him. He was showcasing for your benefit, even if there isn't another checkbook, which there is."

"It makes me sick he's so straight."

Macklin poured an inch of rum into the second glass and sipped it without mixing. He didn't need the jolt, just time to choose his words.

"You've got sixty seconds to tell me why I shouldn't smash that bottle and shove the sharp end through your throat to the spine."

Dorfman looked up from his glass; lifted it and drank it to the bottom, working his throat twice. There was no fear in the gesture. He never drank liquor any other way, doctored or straight from the bottle. He said, "Ahh!", thumped down the glass, and swept the pale moustache off his lip with a finger.

"You wanted a detective. You don't want one smart enough to figure out I'm not repping Mother Teresa?" He thumped the same figure against the table, as if Walker's face were painted on it. "This guy's gone to jail just for keeping his trap shut. In thirty years the cops haven't been able to pry him loose of his client's name. I knew that going in, but I had to make sure he was the same guy I hired years ago. In order to do that I had to give him your name. If he comes back to me saying he'll take the job, he's not the man you want."

"If he's good enough, I can't have him, and if I can have him, he's not good enough?"

"In a nutshell."

A door opened and shut, stirring air in the house. The old woman made a whooshing sound, followed by the noises of outerwear being skinned away.

"Go ahead and talk," Dorfman said. "Last month in temple, Lyla told me she just cut a silent fart, what should she do? I said, 'First of all, change the battery in your hearing aid.' She's a walking confidentiality clause."

But Macklin dropped his voice. "If he's buttoned up too tight to take the job, why are we having this conversation?"

The lawyer laughed, loudly enough for his wife to poke her head into the room. He waved her out and lowered his tone. "You're telling me you always take no for an answer? You?"

He tried Walker's house first. It was a little over half the size of Dorfman's, on the Detroit side of the street that separated the city from Hamtramck, once the traditional enclave of Polish immigrants. Its lines suggested the steep-peaked homes built to shelter assembly-line workers in the early days of Henry Ford's five-dollar-a-day wages. The garage had obviously been constructed after the house next door was razed and the two small lots combined. Once again he parked around the corner and came back on foot. A tall evergreen hedge belonging to the neighbor on the garage side provided a narrow passage where he could peer through the window without being seen. Inside were some tools and an old oil stain where a car had stood. In Detroit more than most places, the absence of a vehicle meant the owner wasn't home.

The wooden window frame needed painting. He slid the blade of his pocketknife between it and the sill and found the latch, a swivel hook that fitted into a metal fastener screwed into the wood. He dug away spongy wood, loosening the fastener, then forced the window up with his hands, tearing free the screws.

Walker kept his garage in good order, but a rainy autumn and winter slush had tracked mud onto the floor that Macklin was careful to avoid lest he leave footprints. A side door that would lead into the house was fastened with a dead bolt. Here was a homeowner who overlooked little; but he might have gone further.

A corner of the garage served as a workshop, with a small bench and an assortment of tools; nothing sophisticated, but one can move worlds with a hammer and screwdriver. Getting around the lock without leaving a gouge or a scratch took time, but he didn't want to put his man on his guard. At last he worked back the bolt, put away the tools, and entered a small kitchen, holding the knife with the blade exposed. He never carried a firearm except when he was working; it could not be explained away like a pocketknife in case he was caught in possession, and the knife itself was virgin. He'd killed his share of men — and women — with knives, but not with this one.

Twenty minutes later he let himself back out the way he'd come, re-engaging the bolt and using the knife to re-seat the window latch, which was altogether more difficult than loosening it had been, and far from perfect. But who apart from a raging paranoid made a daily check of every possible point of entry?

He might have spared himself the trouble of a search, for all he learned of value. A drinking man, Walker, with a half-empty bottle of Old Smuggler in the cupboard above the sink and a lingering iodine odor of Scotch in a glass in the basin. No sign of recent visitors in the living room or bedroom, and all the indications of a man who lived alone and had done so for some time: Only one comfortable chair, overstuffed and worn, a bed with one pillow, basic cable on an old CRT TV set, quite a few books — the man liked John O'Hara — the local cable listings with some movies circled in pencil. No firearms on the premises, but there was a gun-cleaning kit inside the nightstand. The place was no tidier than it had to be, but most of the dishes were washed and the bed was made.

The commute was short to an Edwardian building on Grand River, the downtown corridor, with gryphon-shaped waterspouts and an ancient superintendent with a White Russian accent, mopping the pattern off the linoleum in the foyer. He paid no attention to the visitor who glanced at the snap-letter directory, then started upstairs.

A door with A. WALKER INVESTIGATIONS lettered in black on yellow pebbled glass was unlocked. He paid no attention to the furnishings of a stale waiting room, knocked on a door marked PRIVATE a couple of times, waiting in between, then used his knife to slip the spring lock. The two olive-drab file cabinets were locked, a squat safe too, but he wasn't looking to uncover the

86

man's professional secrets. A charmless desk delivered the usual pencils, paper clips, dust bunnies, and a checkbook that confirmed Dorfman's account of the finances of a business hanging on by its eyebrows. No names of apparent clients. A careful man, at least where work was concerned.

Which was what Macklin had set out to learn.

Walker had doodled on a yellow legal pad, among notations scribbled in a kind of bastard shorthand intended for his eyes only. To the visitor it was just scratches. The wastebasket gave up nothing of value. If he'd kept any record of the assignment that had put him and Macklin in the same building in Toronto at a key moment, it would be locked up; again, it was of no real interest.

He lifted the pad and held it close to his eyes; made out a couple of capital letters followed mostly by lowercase characters that resembled a cardiogram: "De . . . St . . ." Holding it away, he looked again at the doodle. A face, female from the long lashes and curve of the lips, under an old-fashioned cap with a police shield. He remembered the circled listings in Walker's cable TV guide: *He Walked by Night, The Racket, Suddenly.* Nothing filmed later than 1955, all featuring police officers who wore such caps. A crime-movie buff.

"De . . . St . . ." A woman in a police cap.

Deborah Stonesmith, detective lieutenant, Detroit Major Crimes. Macklin knew the name, although they'd never met face-to-face. He let himself back out, locking the door behind him.

His personal car, which he never used for work, was a maroon Chevrolet TrailBlazer, a model the company had discontinued, but there were many still on the road. There in the snow belt, driving an ordinary passenger car was almost a conspicuous act. The engine was a standard six-banger, with all the environmental equipment intact. There was no reason to try to outrun pursuit when he wasn't on business, and certainly no wisdom in raising red flags on computers in squad cars. If he were pulled over and taken in for questioning, Leo Dorfman was a better getaway than the fastest car on the road. He parked six blocks from 1300 Beaubien, fed the meter, and wandered the neighborhood on foot until he spotted the well-used Cutlass.

He used his narrowest blade to slip the lock on the street side of the two-door. The glove compartment carried most of the usual items — minus, of course, the gloves.

A seam underneath the lid hadn't come from the factory. He ran his fingers around the edge, found the small catch, and looked at a Luger with a handle worn almost smooth. He checked the magazine, saw it was fully loaded, slapped shut the extra compartment, and crawled onto the floor of the backseat to wait, holding the pistol loosely to keep his fingers from cramping.

■ ■ ■ ■

ME

■ ■ ■ ■

NINE

The man in the backseat didn't tell me to resist any more stunts like the one I'd tried with the lamppost. Evidently he knew enough about me to know it was unnecessary.

"Gun," he said.

"In the safe at the office. Carrying a piece into the cophouse just makes them mad."

"You'd better be a fast draw if you're lying."

"Is that my spare piece you tickled me with? I thought of finding a better hiding place, but the last time I did that I could only remember where I used to put it."

"Don't kid me it won't fire. It wouldn't be worth keeping as a spare."

"You're Macklin."

"Where can we talk?" He'd withdrawn the gun and sat back a little, but it would still be handy.

This was encouraging. People who are

planning to kill you don't usually engage you in conversation. The chatty villains you see on the screen are rare in life, for obvious reasons.

"We can pull over anywhere," I said.

"I mean face-to-face. The answers you get looking at the back of a man's head don't count."

"A restaurant, then."

"I know you'll feel safer in public, but you might get ideas. I've gone to a lot of trouble just to have to kill you."

"I don't like to cause inconvenience. My office is close."

"Not bad. It's the only one occupied on the top floor."

"You can put away the gun," I said.

"When you put away the car."

For years I'd paid a derelict five bucks to protect my car from vandals like him while it was parked in the empty Cold War gas station across from my building. He'd been shoved out by a pub-style restaurant, but when that failed another homeless entrepreneur had shoved in, hiking the price to ten. Detroit abhors a vacuum.

Holding my Luger inside the slash pocket of a leather windbreaker, Macklin stayed close by my side crossing the street and then the foyer. I got my first good glimpse of him

94

through the corner of my eye. He was about my height, built slighter but not slight, and his profile belonged on the Before side of an advertisement for a male makeover. An ordinarily observant person could forget what he looked like while he was still looking at him. I'm an experienced detective; I held the image until he stepped behind me to climb the stairs.

Rosecranz, the troll who kept the building from sliding into its foundation, knelt on a step halfway to the second floor, scraping petrified gum off the underside of the banister with a stone chisel. He got up to let us pass.

"Is it Leap Year already?" I said.

Macklin and I mounted the last flight without a word.

"Was that necessary?" he said when we reached the top.

"He'd have been suspicious if I didn't say anything. Also I got the satisfaction of hearing your sphincter squeak when I opened my mouth."

"You take chances, Walker."

"Yeah, but you don't."

He confirmed that by throwing me up against the hallway wall and holding me there with a shoulder while he frisked me. All he got was my keys and wallet, and he returned those.

I put my suit back into order and opened the unlocked door to the little waiting room. The only thing waiting there was a ladybug, and it was more interested in the museum-quality copy of *Midwest Living* it was crawling across to pay us any attention. Well, I'd hardly expected the U.S. Cavalry; but a man can hope.

He'd relocked the door to the confession box. A tidy man, Macklin. No archaeologist would find a footprint to show he'd set foot on earth, not in a million years or ten minutes.

Inside the office, he waved me into the swivel behind the desk with the barrel of the Luger, then slid the magazine out of the handle and worked the cigarette-lighter action, kicking the cartridge out of the chamber onto the floor. He laid it atop a file cabinet outside my reach sitting and tried to move the customer's chair closer to the desk, but it wouldn't budge.

"Bolted," he said. "If I hadn't checked the place out I'd expect a gun strapped in the kneehole on your side."

"I'm surprised you missed the bolts. I've got a thing about visitors invading my space, especially when they come here straight from Coney Island with a bellyful of chili and onions. You'd just kill them, I guess."

He sat. "You know me better than that. Lieutenant Stonesmith wants my head on a plate, but she wouldn't lump me in with Jeffrey Dahmer."

I looked at the pad by the telephone and a doodle I hadn't realized I made, of a female face wearing a police cap. "Sigmund Freud, then. I wondered how you got from Leo Dorfman to Thirteen Hundred. You don't have much practice in taking no for an answer, do you?"

"I do. You'd be surprised if I told you how many people try to dicker me down."

"I doubt it. I hear all the time what happens to people who go to cut-rate killers. They almost always turn out to be undercover cops."

He let that line of conversation wither on the vine. Head on, his face was scored deeply from the corners of his nostrils to the corners of his slightly wide mouth. The nose was average like the rest of him, neither big nor small, as straight as it needed to be, and his dark hair was thinning on either side of the widow's peak. The eyes were the giveaway: pale and colorless, shallow as plastic discs, giving up only reflected light. You saw them in cops who should have retired years ago and in psychiatrists whose patients were cases only, no longer people.

And killers.

I slid open the belly drawer — he didn't flinch, but then he'd know what it contained — broke open a pack of cigarettes, tilted it his way. He shook his head, a millimeter each direction. I struck a match off an old burn-canal on the desk and got one going.

It was my turn not to talk. I pushed myself away far enough to sit back and cross my legs, gripping the top ankle the way Brits do in spy novels. I could feel my heart banging all the way down the bone.

He drew a fold of stiff shiny paper from an inside pocket of the windbreaker and put it on the desk within my reach, standing it up like a tent. I dragged on the cigarette, laid it in the tray, scooped up and snapped open the paper. It was good photo stock, the image laser-printed in color. I admired a fresh young face above the roll of a white turtleneck sweater, looking out a window white with frost, cleared as by the heel of a hand in a circle that framed the face, like a halo in a Renaissance painting, a steaming mug nestled between two slim white hands. She wasn't looking at me or anything in particular, and probably not at whoever had taken the picture.

It might have been a model shot for a

fashion magazine, but the legend printed out above and below belonged on a wanted poster.

"Your wife?"

"Yes."

"You got a hundred grand?"

"Ask me a question I'll answer."

"Email, I'm guessing. Any idea who sent it?"

"One."

" 'Just because she doesn't want to live with you doesn't mean you don't want her to live.' Is that true?"

"I wouldn't be here if it weren't."

"Have you warned her?"

"If I did, she'd clear out, and force the issue. Right now she's safe, until he has my answer. Just when he wants it is up to him. He didn't leave contact information, only that 'more soon.' If she moves out, he'll know the answer, and it's out of my hands."

"I guess paying the ransom's not an option."

"You know the playbook. It's just an installment. And it wouldn't guarantee anything. I'm used to final resolutions."

"What do you want me to do?"

"Keep her alive until I can work things out on my end."

"I haven't done bodyguard work in years,

and then it was only because I was broke. It didn't turn out so well for the client."

"I know. I know every case you ever had that made news. I'm just buying time." From the same inside pocket he took a thick envelope, which made a substantial thump when it struck the desk. It was oversize, and packed tight enough to need a rubber band to keep it from splitting; but even so.

I left it where it was. "That's not a hundred grand."

"Fifty. The rest when it's over to my satisfaction."

"It's the satisfaction part that worries me."

He shook his head again. The movement this time was even narrower. "I only kill when I'm paid, or it's in my best interest. You finish what you start — however it turns out — and you play it tight to the vest. I can concentrate knowing Laurie's in capable hands."

"Concentrate on eliminating the threat. What makes it I wouldn't be an accomplice to murder?"

"Nobody's said anything about murder. I'm hiring you to keep an innocent party safe. Where I go from here and what I do, no one can accuse you of knowing."

"Suppose I tell Stonesmith about this meeting."

"I wouldn't. It would move you into the category of my best interest."

I uncrossed my legs and leaned forward to pick up my cigarette. I grabbed the heavy glass tray and scaled it at his head.

He ducked it — I knew then why he conserved his movements so carefully — and beat me to the Luger by a length. Half a second more and the magazine was in place and a fresh cartridge jacked into the chamber.

"You disappoint me," he said.

"I know the feeling."

"What did you hope to accomplish by that?"

"Ounce of prevention. I got bit once by a spider. Now I kill them when I see them."

We returned to our seats. He laid the pistol in his lap. The cigarette was still in my mouth, to my surprise. I drew on it and squashed it out in the canal. I tapped the printout on the desk. "Why don't you just do what you have to do before he makes good on his threat? You can track someone down as well as I can. You proved that in Toronto."

If it was my hole card, I wasted it. Nothing on his face indicated it meant anything. "I'm not a killing machine," he said, "no matter what Stonesmith says. I don't pay tribute, but in certain circumstances I'll give the mark a choice."

"Circumstances such as?"

"Such as the man who sent me that email is my son."

TEN

It was an embarrassing admission by most standards; not his. He spoke as if a family pet had strayed off and killed someone's sheep.

"Roger's mother was my first wife. She died about this time last year. Drank herself to death."

"I wonder why."

"Drunkenness. That's why a drunk drinks. No one can drive them to it. We were divorced for years, but I went to the burial service, for Roger's sake. The cops were there, taking pictures."

"They would."

"We'll get back to that. I didn't realize until then that Roger blamed me for his mother's situation. He threw a punch at me as we were leaving the cemetery."

"Did he connect?"

For answer, Macklin glanced toward the glass ashtray lying where it had landed on the floor.

"The people I used to work for never came to terms with my quitting. They recruited my son. I tried to keep him out. I was sentimental. I should have made it permanent. The fact he's still alive is proof enough he's his father's son."

So far as I could tell there was no pride in the remark; no contempt either, or anything else approaching human emotion. He wasn't a robot, just impossible to read.

"Apart from Dorfman," he said, "Roger was the only one who knew I was divorcing again. He also knows I don't kill for personal reasons. The law doesn't necessarily buy into that; a killer kills, as they see it. If Laurie were murdered, I'd be the immediate suspect. And he'd be sure to plant enough evidence to see I went down for it."

"Thin," I said. "A man in your line makes a new enemy every time he comes through on a contract. And divorce isn't exactly a secret action. Anyone could find out about it, and take advantage of it."

"He knew my email address, another thing he shared with Dorfman."

"What about Dorfman? It wouldn't be the first time a lawyer gave up a shady client with a grand jury barking at his heels."

"Leo helps Leo; that's nothing new in

lawyers, but it fills every minute of his day. But he's too smart to choose sides between the law and me. It's not fear. As old as he is he wants to get to be as old as he can. Anything less would be admitting defeat."

He was getting to be quite the conversationalist.

"Call it instinct on my part," he said, "if you want to fill in the blanks. Anyway I have to run it out, but I need time, which is what I'm buying from you."

"So that's what this is about, saving your skin from a homicide rap involving your estranged wife?"

Something resembling emotion passed across the implacable face, like a dust cloud. It was probably just my imagination. It pleases me to maintain the illusion there's some humanity left in even the worst of the race. In any case he didn't follow up on it, and the impression faded along with my faith that I'd seen anything at all.

"After I left my former employers," he said, "I found out they'd recruited Roger. Some people have an inordinate faith in genes. I did what I could to turn him away. There was collateral damage, but I thought I'd made progress. As it turned out, he is his father's son, with certain inside knowledge of the game.

"That's the other shoe I mentioned earlier. Those police photographers spent as much time on Roger as they did on me. When I saw that, I knew he was still active." He frowned down at the pistol on his lap, then put it on the desk, just far enough outside my reach to react. "I think he's capable of holding me to account for what he thinks I did to his mother."

"But not so much he wouldn't take a hundred G to forgive the debt."

"That's one of the questions I want to ask him, before I make my decision."

I rose from my chair, without asking permission; I paid the rent, after all. His only answer was to rest a hand on the Luger. I unlocked the safe, keeping far enough away from the opening so he could see what I was doing, reached past the .38 Chief's Special lying there, and scooped out the bottle of Dewar's I kept for company, mostly mine. Again I offered him a hit; this time he nodded, taking up no more space than when he shook his head.

I took two pony glasses from the safe. "Water? No ice, sorry. A refrigerator would blow the building's circuits."

Another head shake. I filled the glasses and held one out. He sat unmoving with his hands in his lap on either side of the Luger until I set the drink down inside his reach. When I was in my chair holding mine he picked his up and drank the top off it.

"You've got better taste in the office than you do at home."

"I hope *that* lock gave you more trouble."

"If you're thinking you don't have a choice in this," he said, "you don't. I've told you as much as I had to, which is too much. If things fall that way and you hear about the untimely death of one Roger Macklin, I can't afford to let you run around with that burden on your conscience."

"What makes it less costly if I take the job and that happens?"

"*Then* a hungry prosecutor might charge you as an accessory. So you'll bury your conscience along with your civic pride."

I made myself sip my Scotch. I didn't care if he saw me take it down in a lump, but I wanted the time to figure out how to crawl inside the glass and roll it out the window. The chance of surviving the three-story fall beat all the options. When it was empty I slipped the rubber band off the envelope, separated fifteen bills from the sheaf of hundreds, and slid it back his way.

"My retainer," I said. "I never charge more than that unless the job takes more than three days. I'm not Gandhi; if Roger slips and falls into the path of a bullet, ten years' salary showing up in my possession is as good as a smoking gun. It's a security job, that's all."

If that face could show surprise, I was a witness. He frowned and put away the envelope.

He spent ten minutes telling me everything he knew about his ex-bride-to-be. Most husbands don't know that much, and he was no exception, so far as their married life was concerned, but he was as good as Google when it came to her background before they met. Of course he'd have checked her as far back as the womb before proposing. Where a man who makes his living by killing is concerned, the woman in his life has no mystery.

"What's my cover?" I said. "If I tell her I'm working for you, she'll spook and holler cop."

"She doesn't spook. But if she balks, say 'Leroy.' "

I repeated the name. I knew better than to ask who Leroy was. You get only so many breaths in this life and there was no use wasting one on a question he wouldn't answer.

Once again he drew the pistol's fangs and rose. "I'll leave this in the other room. Don't be in any great hurry to go through the door."

I sat back cradling my drink. "How do I know when the job's done?"

"No one's ever had to ask me that before." He went out, shutting the door behind him.

When I heard the hall door close, I put down the glass and swiveled toward the safe to unlock it. The Luger is a stopgap, better than no gun at all but no match for most: The Rube Goldberg action lacks the reliability of German engineering at its best. I took out the Chief's Special revolver, holster and all, swung out the cylinder for a look-see, and clipped it to my belt. For the foreseeable future it would be my conjoined twin.

I retrieved the Luger, reassembled it, and locked it in the safe. I didn't run into Rosecranz on the way out; not that he'd have pumped me for information. He'd left his curiosity at the Brandenburg Gate.

The address Macklin had given me for his wife was burning a hole in my pocket. When I entered the dank gray deserted building across the street, the man who'd appointed himself to look after the Cutlass scrambled up off his straw pallet and stood yawning and rubbing his stomach. He couldn't be that tired and there wasn't that much stomach to rub. I sighed and cracked open my wallet.

"No, sir; I was just surprised you wanted the car again so fast."

The *sir* threw me. I took a closer look at him. He wasn't dressed for a charity ball, but apart from being worn and several cycles past due washing, his clothes wouldn't get him turned out by the elbow. He was younger than I'd thought at first — eighteen or twenty — and less septic, his shoulder-length hair glossy black and his face clean except for some bits of lint from the pallet caught in his chin-whiskers. His teeth decided the thing: too white for the street and too even to have come in that way outside the supervision of an orthodontist. I'd have realized he wasn't the same man I'd been dealing with if I hadn't been preoccupied earlier; try testing your own powers of concentration with an armed killer at your side.

"You're not a tramp." I put away the wallet, but left my thumb hooked in my hip pocket, alongside the Chief's Special. "Not the career kind. Runaway?"

"No, sir! I'm an urban explorer."

"What the hell's an urban explorer?"

"People with an interest in the history of a place. We go into abandoned houses, closed garages, boarded-up businesses, collecting impressions of the people who came before us."

"And what else?"

"Nothing. Just impressions."

"This place has been empty only a couple of months. The impression I get is of bad management and a rotten location."

"I got that after five minutes. I'm just crashing. My parents think I'm in Fort Lauderdale. They'd rather think I'm boozing on the beach than poking around old buildings, especially in Detroit. They're in Grosse Pointe Woods."

Twenty minutes from downtown and an age away.

"Anything juicy so far?"

A lower lip got pushed out. "A body, last month. In a condemned parking structure. Turned out to be a hooker. Somebody cut her throat and also —" He flushed. I'd thought that had gone out with panty raids. I was in danger of liking him.

"They can't all be King Tut." I almost snarled it. "How many of you are there?"

He frowned, stroked his whiskers, picked fluff from them. "Hundreds, maybe. I don't know them all. Sometimes I meet with the ones I do know and we go in together." He dug a cell phone out from under his plaid shirt. "If any of the others are like me, they go in alone as much as not."

"What do you do with these impressions?"

"I don't know about the others, but I'm writing a thesis." He spread his palms. " 'Digging up Detroit: Archaeological Studies of the Modern City.' "

"You're a college student?"

"Wayne State. I'm on winter break."

"What's your name, or should I call you Indiana?"

He showed his excellent orthodontia. "Dr. Chuck."

"Doctor?"

"I mean, when I get my Ph.D."

"What's with the shakedown, Chuck?"

"What's a shakedown?"

He made me tired. I'd have to fill him in every time just to have an argument.

"The ten bucks you soaked me to garage this heap. It won't pay back your student loan."

"That's what I had to pay the man who usually looks after this building to let me fill in for him. You want it back?" He fumbled under his plaid tail.

"I already charged it to expenses. If you're here, where's he?"

"One of his other places, I guess. He says he's got a string of 'em, vacant lots and like that, where people can find parking without having to walk a mile."

"A franchise on real estate nobody wants. Only in Detroit. Urban explorers, you said? Much obliged." I got my wallet back out and gave him five.

The whites of his eyes shone in the gloom. "What's it for?"

"Teaching me something new. That's fee simple in my work."

"Thanks, Mr. — ?"

I gave him a card. "Next good impression you get, let me know. I'm a collector myself. Meanwhile, watch your back, Doc. A cop might take you for a scrap rat, or a scrap rat for another scrap rat, and then it's 'Digging up Chuck.' "

I left him putting away the bill; to him, another treasure from the city's hollowed-out past.

My tail showed up on schedule, the only really reliable service in our city. I spotted it after three blocks; but then I was looking for it. I made out two heads in the front seat of a brushed-gold four-door and wondered when the Detroit Police Department had converted its unmarked rolling stock from Ford to Chevy.

Eleven

A police shadow isn't as easy to shake as you see in movies. Cops are the creative consultants, after all, and they don't sell their secrets that cheap.

Most of the time I humor them; otherwise they get unreasonable, and I like to see my tax dollars at work. Not this time. Deb Stonesmith had been too eager to find out where Laurie Macklin had landed, and if it wasn't my secret to share in her office it still wasn't on the road.

I took I-75 north of the city, my fall-back place when I want to be alone. I timed it just far enough ahead of rush hour to slide into a pocket but not so far ahead I couldn't shut the door behind me with a few hundred tons of Detroit steel. When I bailed out at the exit to the zoo, I left the unmarked Chevy stuck between a pair of Wide Load house movers and a flatbed steelhauler, with concrete walls twelve feet high on either side

114

designed as part of a drainage ditch in times of flood. I doubled back to I-96 West.

Stonesmith hadn't actually said that Laurie Macklin had "vanished" from Southfield — magic is lost on cops — but if she had, she wouldn't have been exaggerating by much. If you want to vanish from any place within a twenty-minute drive of Detroit, you can't do much better than Milford, the Town Time Forgot.

They don't write it up often. No one famous was born there, and nothing of particular historical interest has ever happened within its limits; but that doesn't stop similarly unremarkable places from being gushed over in print. There seemed to be a conspiracy to keep this one a secret from the despoiling multitudes.

It's a village of around five thousand, roughly fifteen miles west of Detroit's fastest-growing suburb, and a solid eighty years back in time. The main four corners is just that, a once-upon-a-time place anchored by four stories of former furniture store and settled by wheelwrights and boilermakers in scale-model miniatures of robber barons' palaces in Old New York. The people who live there now commute between Detroit and the university town of Ann Arbor thirty minutes west, and when they exit the Walter P. Chrysler freeway they pass through a time warp. I felt the shockwave myself, and I was just visiting.

The big snows were yet to come. What remained of the first made half-moons in depressions in the lawns, frozen hard as plaster and edged with yellow where little boys — and some probably not so little — had tried to melt them before their bladders ran dry. It was one of those places where that was still a game and not a misdemeanor.

The house wasn't as large as the Cabot Inn or as ornate, but the modest millionaire who'd built it about the same time had employed contractors who remembered how much fun it was to play hide-and-seek. Amid its dormers and bump-outs a child with an ordinary imagination could find niches in sufficient number and variety to wait out any adult's store of patience. At one time, it would have been a paint-seller's dream of pinks, teals, aquas, vermilions, peaches, and daffodils, but a later occupant had slapped gray on top of it all, adding white trim in a fit of artistic daring. That would have been around the time the house was parsed out into single-dweller suites.

It had three stories plus an attic. Laurie Macklin lived on the third. I recognized the window she'd looked out through whilst warming her hands around a steamy mug, unaware her picture was being taken. I shook out a cigarette, turned my back to the wind, and cupped a match in my hands. While I pretended to concentrate on that, I drew a sight line between the window and the little community park across the street. A gazebo of pressure-treated pine stood square in its dead center, with latticework around the base to keep out small animals. It was just the thing to hide behind while poking a lens through one of the diamond-shaped openings where the slats crossed.

He wouldn't still be there. Why should he? Even blackmailers took time off. But I didn't tarry. I flipped the cigarette into the gutter after one puff and mounted the steps to the front porch, where a row of bleeding hearts had bled out their lives in pots on the railing. Their shriveled blooms dangled over the sides like shrunken heads.

The door wasn't locked; that would have been redundant. It led into a foyer that no longer bore any resemblance to the ground floor of a private house. A partition had been built a few steps in, studded with labeled brass mailboxes and a circular mesh grid assigned to each. Another door, this one with a Judas window, separated me from the rest of the house.

I'd rehearsed and discarded several cover stories during the drive there. If she was as cagy as Stonesmith let on, none would get me past the door. If she heard me out and turned me down flat, I could opt out. Provided this client let me.

A card next to 310 read L. ZIEGLER. Macklin had told me to look for his wife under that name. I pushed the button.

"Who is it, please?"

A voice just above middle register, not more than the usual challenge in it.

"Amos Walker, Ms. Ziegler. I'm a private investigator."

A brief pause.

"Is it about my husband?"

So much for the incognito. I wondered why she bothered.

"I'm here on his behalf."

"Did Leo Dorfman hire you?"

"No, I'm working directly for Macklin."

"Are you here to kill me?"

She might have asked if I had a package to be signed for.

I grinned at the intercom. "Why would a plumber pay someone else to fix the drain?"

More dead air. "Hang on."

Something buzzed and the door went clunk. I swung it open and climbed a steep staircase between lime-green walls.

There was a window at each end of the hall on her floor with the kind of view they sell in the Home Décor section at Target: barber poles, bike racks, front porches, and bandstands. All the ice cream trucks were in mothballs until April. I pushed the button next to 310 and looked at a .32 pistol.

It was a Davis with a light wood handle and a brushed-steel finish and nested nicely in her right hand. It was a slim hand, the nails unpainted but neatly rounded. They belonged to a smallish ash-blonde with her hair cut at an angle with her jaw, cloudy blue eyes, and good skin. She looked younger than her picture; too young for me, and for that matter her husband. Her quilted robe matched her eyes. A pair of slightly darker open-toed slippers poked out from under the hem. Those nails too were tended and not painted. She had long slender feet with high arches, a feature often neglected by good-looking women.

That she had tensile strength was something sensed rather than seen, and probably inherited, a kind of confidence in her bearing. It had nothing to do with the gun; most women, in fact, and as many men, are as nervous behind one as they are in front of it.

"Unbutton your jacket," she said.

I did.

"Turn around and lift the tail."

I did that. When I was facing her again she said, "Where's your gun?"

"Downstairs in the car. I've been to Milford before. I've never had to shoot my way out."

"I suppose you have an ID of some kind."

I unshipped the folder, taking my time. The little pistol stayed level and she'd given herself plenty of room to move. Her eyes stayed on my face for another beat, then flicked to the license and the sheriff's star for a nanosecond.

"Is that real?"

"The license is. The badge cost me six box tops."

"I don't know what that means."

"Wrong crowd. Too young. The badge means nothing. The county hands them out like party favors when you serve papers to people who don't want them."

"Are you always this funny?"

"Funnier, usually. Do you want to shoot me here or wait till you get home?"

"I am home."

"Lady, you're killing me. Whoops. Poor choice of words."

Something tugged at the corners of her

lips. It didn't stay long. She'd picked up that trick from her husband. Picked up more than that, probably. I'd never seen anyone more comfortable with death in her hand.

She moved for the first time since she'd opened the door: Thumbed the safety catch on, slipped the pistol into a blue quilted pocket, stepped back to let me pass. As I did I caught a tinge of scented soap and warm skin. I seemed to be spending a lot of time lately interrupting women in the shower.

It was a pleasant living room, lit from behind a soffit and by a winter sun as murky as dishwater. Red and yellow lozenges decorated a rug that fell two feet shy of the walls, leaving the floor exposed, eight-inch maple planks fitted as tight as when they were laid. There were books and magazines on an apostrophe-shaped coffee table with three legs. The walls were painted in semi-gloss eggshell, bouncing light evenly around the room.

She sat in a space-age wing chair uphol-stered in red leather, crossing her legs. I perched on the edge of a sofa covered in something smooth and porous decorated with rectangles.

"What's on Peter's mind?" she said. "I

expected to hear directly from Dorfman before this."

"This doesn't have to do with the divorce. I'm supposed to keep you alive until Macklin can defuse a threat against your life." I told her the rest. Her expression didn't change until I mentioned Macklin's son.

"Roger? We've never met. All I know about him is what Peter told me. He was pretty sure he'd gotten the boy free from mob influence."

"Maybe he was. Maybe he's right. But Peter got himself free too — without changing his occupation."

"Roger's a grown man now. I think he's a year older than I am. Do you think he resents me?"

"No more than a hundred grand's worth, if it isn't just a dodge. Your husband thinks he wants to squeeze him for abandoning his mother, then torture him by killing you."

"Some abandonment. My lawyer's using the settlement Peter made on her as a basis for negotiation."

"You're a cool customer, Mrs. Macklin. Most women would at least blink when told they're a target. Most men, too. Some in Macklin's own line of work."

"I've had practice." She dandled a foot, her first sign of agitation. If that's what it was. You can read anything into body language. "If it's all the same to you, I'll arrange my own protection."

"Leroy."

"What?" But she'd heard me. Her face paled around the edges.

"Something Macklin said to tell you, if you turned me down."

"Did he tell you what it means?"

"No."

"Then it means nothing." Her color had come back.

"Okay." I stood.

Her gaze followed me up. "You don't put up much of a fight."

"I don't want the job. He didn't give me the choice of refusing."

"How much was he offering?"

"He mentioned an amount. I used it as a basis for negotiation."

She rose. "Thank you, Mr. Walker. I'm not a fool. I know when I've been warned."

"I can recommend some people who specialize in this kind of work."

"That's kind of you, but I have a network of my own. It might surprise you the contacts one makes when she's married to a man like Peter."

"I'll leave this just in case." I got out a card and laid it on the tripod table.

"Incidentally, I'm Lauren Ziegler here. My maiden name is Ziegenthaler. I don't enjoy entertaining the police."

"I thought it was something like that."

I saw something as I crossed in front of the window looking out on the street, or thought I did; a movement near the gazebo in the park. I didn't turn my head to confirm it. It may be the work, but when I feel someone's watching me I'm right more often than I'm wrong.

And I knew then this wasn't going to be a job I could get fired from so easily.

TWELVE

I didn't glance toward the park on my way back to the car. I knew what I'd seen, and even more what I'd felt, and there was everything to lose by spreading it around.

I drove aimlessly, admiring the Victorian and Edwardian houses in the neighborhood, the frozen American flags hanging as stiff as galvanized sheets from their staffs, counting the bicycles and basketball hoops. A nice community, on the surface. In ancient times and in other places the city fathers had erected walls around them to keep things that way.

When I got tired of that I ate a sandwich in a tavern in the little downtown area, a place with pewter steins on a shelf above the bar, drank two beers, and went back to the car to light a cigarette. Then I drove back to the park, this time along the street on the other side. The slots were deserted that time of day at that time of year, and I had my choice. I finished smoking and ditched the butt when I got out.

The grass was still green; the light snow covering had insulated it from the cold without killing it, but it crunched underfoot like the fake kind they put in Easter baskets. A set of footprints showed clearly going in the opposite direction from mine. I'm no Daniel Boone, but the temperature was climbing above freezing so they couldn't have been there more than a few minutes, and the same tracks, roughly a man's size ten, had been made in the paper-thin layer of frost that slicked the wooden planks that made up the floor of the gazebo.

The man who belonged to them had stood for a while in front of the railing across from the window I'd passed in front of; he'd changed positions a few times, overlapping his own prints, before turning and leaving.

That was as much as I could get. Whether he'd just looked or took time to take some more pictures — possibly of me — I could only guess. I had to guess he'd brought his camera, but it didn't matter either way. I'd been made, or would be soon.

Well, it had to happen sometime. An invisible bodyguard isn't much of a deterrent. I'd just hoped, if the job came about, I'd be settled in and ready before I got famous.

Now I'd run out of time.

I was still employed, whether Laurie Macklin approved or not.

The Chief's Special rode heavy next to my right kidney. It wouldn't be back in the safe or in its other place in the niche under the glove compartment for a while. Apart from the change of clothes and indestructible provisions I keep in the car for emergencies, it was as much luggage as I'd had the opportunity to pack.

He'd go straight to Macklin, his son or whoever he was if not him, probably upping the ante, and when that didn't work he'd be back here to prove he wasn't out just for fun. Whatever I thought of professional killers, or for that matter the women who put up with them, standing pat wasn't an option.

I left the car where it was, crossed through the park on foot, and buzzed 310 again from the foyer.

She was expecting me. Probably she'd seen me from her window coming across the street. "What now?"

I wasn't alone. A woman with the face of a born widow, sour and suspicious, was unlocking the mailbox next to hers. Her cloth coat smelled like onions. The ear nearest me was cocked forward like a German shepherd's.

"Another minute of your time," I said into the speaker.

"What difference would another minute make?"

"Maybe none. Maybe plenty."

"Come ahead, then."

This time I didn't see the pistol, but her right hand rested in the pocket of the blue robe. She had the door open just wide enough for me to see that.

I said, "I think you'd better tell me about Leroy."

Him

THIRTEEN

The important thing to remember was not to treat the mark different from all the others.

"Target practice. That's all they are."

The man who'd taught him that — who'd taught him everything he knew that he hadn't learned from experience — was long dead, by his own protégé's hand, but the proof of his words was in the way he'd died. In the end, Macklin's mentor was target practice, nothing more. Anger, anguish, sorrow, pride, all the things that came with betrayal, were unnecessary distractions. Macklin had disposed of him like tissue.

He assembled a file as he had with all the others, from family albums, medical reports, school yearbooks —

Roger's first tooth.

He peeled it from the adhesive Donna had used all those years ago to add it to the scrapbook, rolled the jagged little thing between thumb and forefinger and stuck it back down. It was just an exercise, repeated many times, and each time it was connected to a dead man. He placed little store in psychic vibrations. Personal contact brought him that much closer to the target.

Seated in the Warren living room with the blinds drawn, he paged through the big three-ring binder, removing those items he considered useful and laying them side by side on the coffee table: Roger's kindergarten photo, smiling with lips pressed tight in the garish cowboy shirt his mother had picked out for the all-important session; a snap of a somewhat sullen adolescent sorting through a handful of pebbles on the shore of Lake Superior; a graduating high-school senior wearing his first suit and tie, good-looking enough but not as handsome as his smug expression seemed to announce. A grainy telephoto shot, this time in a different suit and dark glasses, hands folded at his waist at his mother's graveside. A contact had smuggled that one out of the MacNamara Federal Building in Detroit.

The rest — including the medical file, which included only information gathered during the marriage — had come to him in a thick padded envelope ten days after Donna's funeral, by way of the same legal firm she'd retained to represent her in the divorce. There had been no note included other than a letter typed on the firm's stationery, explaining their late client had made arrangements to send the material to him upon her death.

There would be no sentimentality involved. It was her way of reminding him of what he'd thrown away, grinding guilt in with her heel. It said a good deal about her, about her inability to let go of a grudge, and of her lack of understanding of the man with whom she'd spent seventeen years of her life. He'd put aside any regrets in the relief of their parting at last, and with so few ramifications; her attorney, in his greed to own a substantial part of the money Macklin had made from fulfilling mortal contracts, had neglected to report what his client had told him to the police. In the end, all it had cost was money. Replacing it had been no challenge. His services were always in demand.

True, he'd still felt some responsibility for Roger, and when he learned that Macklin's former employers had chosen his son to fill his vacancy (their faith in genetics was almost touching), he'd risked death to turn him from that path. That settled — or so he'd hoped — he'd ignored his own instincts and attended Donna's burial, exposing himself to police and FBI photographers and expanding his official file. When Roger responded by trying to knock him down, Macklin knew he'd discharged all his responsibilities, with interest.

Not because of anger. He'd learned early to keep uncontrollable emotions in a kind of lock box. And certainly not because of pain. However adept his son was with edged and percussion weapons, his idea of hand-to-hand combat was a John Wayne–style roundhouse right at an obliging chin. Macklin had seen it coming like a slow-moving truck. He could have ducked it entirely, let the young fool stumble and fall on his face in front of an audience of mourners, but out of some lingering sense of — what, paternal debt? More likely it was to avoid a long, drawn-out campaign of unresolved revenge — he'd let the blow glance along his jaw, leaving a colorful bruise but no real discomfort. It gave satisfaction to the boy and closure to the man.

Or so he'd thought.

If Macklin had a professional failing, it was that he assumed everyone who thrived in his occupation avoided human feelings like the flu. When he learned through the grapevine that Roger had resumed doing wet work, he assumed that time and experience had taught him to leave things as they lay beside his mother's plot and get on with business.

Macklin's own contacts in law enforcement had been of the same opinion. Their superiors had dared to hope that Roger would now "turn" and inform on his father. Cops on the beat and agents in the field had picked him up and used all their psychology, but were neither disappointed nor surprised when he laughed in their faces. But when the transcripts reached Macklin, he read between the lines and knew nothing had changed.

When Laurie told him that Roger had called asking after Peter, and that she'd said they were separating and seeking a divorce, he'd suspected the worst.

Which was what had happened.

Their decision to end the marriage was mutual, and far from rancorous. Macklin's courtship intentions of leaving the Life behind him had failed; it would not leave him. He hadn't expected her to live with that truth. Who would, having the ability to choose? He did not. And he was grateful for the warning, although he wished she'd been more circumspect about their situation.

But it would have been unreasonable to

expect otherwise. She hadn't had his practice in the art of dissembling, or for that matter the need to study. He'd dug this hole and now it was up to him to get her out of it.

After the email came demanding ransom in return for sparing her, he'd wasted time ticking through his list of enemies. Most he'd killed, which was what you did with enemies rather than collect them like autographs. Some were in prison, and would be until they left in boxes or in wheelchairs with oxygen tanks onboard. While that wouldn't have stopped them from hiring out the work, he rejected that explanation.

There was no percentage in revenge, and in every convict's heart lurked the hope of parole. The slightest shadow on their record of good behavior would destroy that. The rest were at large and had been for a long time after he'd given them reason to wish him extinct. Too long. If they were ever going to strike they'd have done it by now.

Even that was time squandered. The only person, apart from Leo Dorfman and Laurie, who knew Macklin didn't "want to live with her" was Roger. He should have seen that right away. It made him furious — but only with himself. He hadn't the luxury of directing it anywhere else.

He turned again to the medical report. Dorfman, he knew, could use his own contacts to obtain more recent information, but there were things of interest in the old file that might be of advantage. At ten, following a season of fatigue, night sweats, and joint pain during which the boy's grades had fallen, Donna had taken him to a pediatrician, who'd ordered tests and X-rays and diagnosed rheumatic fever. Bed rest and an aggressive treatment involving antibiotics, cortisone, and related steroids over the summer break had restored him to normal, so that with some remedial education he'd been able to rejoin his class without missing a grade. Regular checkups had failed to note any significant damage to the heart valves.

Now, Macklin's search online revealed that without daily doses of penicillin, sulfomides, and other antibiotics, recurrent attacks were a possible danger. These could lead to endocarditis, a bacterial infection threatening the health of the aortic valve, the tricuspid valve, and the aorta itself, which if not treated early made the victim susceptible to a coronary attack or, transmitted by blood, to kidney failure, renal shutdown, and probably death.

In the normal course of events, Donna would have done whatever was necessary to prevent the worst; but sometime during Roger's adolescence, her social drinking had escalated to alcoholism. Macklin didn't know just when she'd begun to suspect that her husband's retail camera business was a blind, or when she learned the rest; but not long after their son turned seventeen, she'd entered into divorce proceedings. Macklin couldn't be sure, because his work — his real work — had taken him away from home for weeks at a time, leaving such things as medical appointments to her, but it was possible that in the whiskey fog she'd lived in, they fell into neglect. Roger might not have received the treatment he needed to recover completely.

At the very least, chronic serious illness put Roger at a disadvantage in any violent confrontation. On the other end of the spectrum, it could be the instrument of his removal.

Macklin put aside the report, removed his reading glasses, and tapped the side bows against his chin. He'd shot many, cut the throats of as many more, garroted some, bludgeoned others, and shed blood in just about all the ways one creature could shed another's; but in the one-third of his life he'd spent ending other men's (and some women's) lives, helping someone toward natural death was something new.

It bore consideration; but not until Dorf-man came through with more recent up-dates on his son's physical condition.

In the meanwhile, the man himself needed to be located.

The pictures he'd posted of Laurie, care-fully laid out in chronological order accord-ing to season, suggested that Roger had established himself in a place convenient to her access. Like his father, he'd learned not to leave a paper trail; which in view of the world security condition had made the practice of traveling under false names nearly impossible. He certainly wouldn't fly commercial airlines with the frequency required if he were living more than a few hundred miles away, the rails were govern-ment property and as such their surveillance was an unacceptable hazard, and even the bus companies trained their drivers to take note of regular passengers. For all the lip service their representatives gave public transportation, U.S. residents still traveled mainly by private automobile.

But even that posed a problem to those who sought invisibility. Cars needed service and refueling, and garages and filling sta-tions were under the same camera scrutiny as banks and prisons, trained to take in license plates as well as vehicles and drivers. One could never be sure that some overzealous federal agent wasn't putting in hundreds of hours of overtime comparing footage and tracking how many times a particular motorist showed his face or his registration number along the same route. No, despite the fact that Macklin had neither encouraged nor trained his son to follow the lethal trade, he'd inherited enough common sense to limit the distance of his commute.

Any tracker knows the best way to pick up a trail is to go to the last place where the game was known to have been. Macklin, who had gone to Laurie's new house out of curiosity after she'd given his divorce attorney to send papers, had recognized the window where she'd been standing nursing a mug of coffee when Roger took the most recent picture he'd sent. He'd hardly have left anything behind, but the gazebo in the little village park would be the best place to center the spiral of his search.

He drove the TrailBlazer to Milford, parked three blocks away and around the corner from Laurie's apartment, and was walking along a street on the other side of the park when he spotted the beat-up blue Cutlass parked directly opposite the gazebo. He stopped, looked at the erect figure of the man standing under its roof staring at the apartment window. He reversed directions toward the cover of the SUV.

Driving away, he considered what he'd seen. He'd instructed Walker to seek out Laurie, not Roger. But what else could he be doing, standing on the identical spot where his son had drawn his photographic bead on Macklin's wife?

And whose idea was it, really, for him to hire the detective, his or Walker's? And on whose behalf?

In a convenience store–service station near the on-ramp to I-96, he found that rarity, a public telephone, and spent some money. When Leo Dorfman came on, he said, "How soon can you get hold of Amos Walker's medical file?"

■ ■ ■

THEM

■ ■ ■

FOURTEEN

The woman never had visitors.

It might have been different back in Southfield, where she was established, with a husband and a supermarket she liked well enough to shop there twice a week, in the kind of neighborhood whose residents talked to one another when they met on the street; not here in this jerkwater Gomerville, where she was unknown. Despite what you saw on Nick at Nite, all those sappy-sweet small-town sitcoms, the locals closed ranks against strangers. It was the same as being the new kid in school. In the months he'd been watching her and taking her picture, no one else had entered her apartment, not even a cleaning lady. She took care of things herself, dragging a vacuum back and forth in front of the window facing the park, Lemon-Pledging, the whole Mrs. Brady bit, only without Alice the housekeeper. Cooked for herself.

Which infuriated him. The kind of money Macklin brought in, an amount that likely would increase once there was a judgment — if not alimony, then surely a fat settlement based on the not inconsiderable income he declared on his taxes — she could afford a full-time staff, and better living arrangements in a city with life in it, none of this shit-kicking Saturday night Bingo in the VFW hall. What was the opposite of pretentious? And was it any less hypocritical than flaunting one's advantages?

He shook his head. *They're just target practice;* who'd told him that? Not his father, that phony who'd brought up his son to respect the legitimate world that he himself only visited occasionally, to keep up the lousy front. Carlo Maggiore? Possibly; although if so he'd probably just been repeating a line he'd heard from someone who had imagination. That was the failing that had led to Maggiore's death, no imagination or ability to envision the possibility that he'd die anywhere other than in his bed, ninety and rich. But, no, he wouldn't be quit on, not the Don. And so he himself had wound up just target practice, and it was Roger's father who'd done it, only with a blade across the throat instead of the bul-

146

let Roger had in mind for his beloved stepmother, instant and humane.

Target practice. No malice in the act. Gloat later.

Mercy wasn't in it, and hatred was disastrous. When the time came, whether Peter Macklin bore the ignominy of buying Laurie's life or refused, Roger would dispatch the man who'd sired him with no emotion at all. That was the old man's method. Let him experience it from the receiving end. Roger didn't care about the money; he had plenty of his own, earned the same way. He just wanted to see the old man bleed twice.

Again he shook himself, to clear his brain of reflection and projection. Laurie Macklin had a visitor. Roger had arrived at his old post in the park too late to see him arrive, but had caught a glimpse of him passing the window on his way out of the apartment, moving too swiftly to leave anything more than an impression of size and gender.

He'd thought of withdrawing before the man emerged from the building lest he be seen, but that would leave the thing in mystery. His patience paid off minutes later. A tall, broad-shouldered figure in a winter-weight blue suit came out; a man older than his father, favoring one leg as he climbed into a car that needed body work. It was one of those old models with a long low profile and most likely a herd of wild horses under the hood. The man never once glanced toward the park, and when the motor started with a deep-throated rumble and rolled away with a blat of glass-pack pipes, Roger raised his phone and tried for a shot of the license plate, but it was gone before he could focus.

That would slow things down, but not by much. How many of those cars were on the road? Too many, considering the proximity of the Motor City, where rusty hulks were revered on the same level as dead world champions, emaciated Motown musicians, and any huckster who promised to turn a crack house into a sports stadium — with taxpayers' assistance. But there in the rust belt, most of the muscle cars of antiquity hibernated through the winter under canvas, in heated garages, like premature babies in incubators. Those who exposed them to snow, sleet, slush, hail, and salt did so only because they had no other means of transportation. That narrowed the field; and although Roger Macklin had yet to build the network of inside information that Peter Macklin had developed over twenty years, he had some resources.

He may not yet be in his father's tax

bracket — if there was such a thing for their way of making a living — but he had tens of thousands of dollars at his disposal; and the civil servants who hadn't as much as a thousand at theirs were always open to reason.

One thing experience had taught him was not to linger in one place long enough to invite attention. As soon as the car was out of sight he left the gazebo, exiting the park by a different route from the one he'd taken on the way in. The sun, its existence taken on faith alone for days, opened a rift in the overcast; any traces he'd left on the frosted grass would be gone soon.

Not that anyone in Milford would connect a casual stroller with the feral things that prowled the streets of big bad Detroit.

His car was a blue Corvette, bought used. He could afford brand new, but cash transactions that size raised red flags. Many of the old-timers, his father included, shied from the flash of a sports car; but what good was money if all you did was bale it up and bury it? The cockpit-like interior, all brown leather with wood trim on the dash, served as his office, with a PC he'd had custom installed and a hands-free phone. He could take over a company or a small nation at eighty miles per hour.

He tugged on his driving gloves, straddled his shades on his nose, and turned the key. The big 400 started with the same full-throated growl as Mr. X's Cutlass; there might be more there than met the eye, and probably more surprises under the cheap suit and behind the bum leg.

He spoke a number aloud, heard the dial tone, and pulled away from the curb; spending too much time so close to a target ran against his principles. His party picked up as he was pulling into the parking lot of a family restaurant.

The conversation was brief, and conducted without names. He provided a description of the man and the car.

"Michigan plate, that's all you got?"

"Hey, if I had the number, I wouldn't be calling you. Start with the insurance companies, get the names of year-around customers who drive those jalopies. Most of the bozos only cover them from March to November, then put 'em up on blocks. If they took care of pussy the way they take care of their wheels they wouldn't have so much to prove." He cut the connection.

It might be a wild-goose chase. The sturdily built stranger who'd made his way into Laurie Macklin's tight circle might be no more than one of those opportunists who

150

live on grass widows and a gift of gab; in which case he was no threat. But if he'd learned anything from his father's example, *this* Macklin knew that when a ball came from left field you dove for it.

PATIENT PLAN
Walker, Amos (no middle)
Reason(s) for Visit
Follow-up GSW
Condition: Extensive damage of the superficial fascia describing oblique canal bisecting superficial nerves and vessels, bypassing femoral artery approx. 2 cms. to right
Assessment: Scarring in canal impeding muscle movement, p. chronic
Impression: Vicodin and all opioids n.r. because of previous abuse; aspirin, ibuprofen, acetaminophen r. as needed, not to exceed twelve in twelve hours

That was the latest, and the one of most interest to Macklin. A much older report referred to an earlier gunshot wound to the lower thorax, requiring surgery to repair a compound fracture of two anterior ribs. In all likelihood, arthritis would slow him down in damp weather, but not so much as the permanent injury to his leg. He'd taken

151

a 30.06 slug — a deer round — through the upper thigh, plowing a canal all the way through to a clean exit, missing the femoral artery by a whisker; otherwise he'd have bled out before the fastest ambulance could arrive on the scene. During and after recovery he'd overmedicated with Vicodin, which together with a taste for alcohol (other medical reports were as informative as they were objective) had placed him temporarily in a rehabilitation center, without his consent; a case of legal committal.

Instinct based on personal contact told Macklin the last would be of no use to him. A man who was still a slave to drugs didn't handle straight Scotch so well. The leg wound was important; if it came to physical combat, a blow to the thigh would paralyze him with pain long enough to deliver a *coup de grace.*

Other older reports were revealing and, for someone not as schooled in the variables of the human condition, puzzling. The patient had suffered multiple concussions — which, if one took into account those that might have gone unreported — should have incapacitated him years ago: dementia, Parkinson's, epilepsy, cerebral hemorrhage for starters. But like certain automobiles, some individuals were built to take more abuse than others that had come off the same line; a screw tightened an extra quarter-turn in the factory, an additional thirty-second of an inch thickness occurring in the occipital bone in the womb, or just plain luck in the angle and severity of impact. Based on their brief meeting, here was one model with all the important parts in working order.

A challenge, if it came to a confrontation.

Macklin tipped the printouts Dorfman had provided back into the folder, carried it into his kitchen, and after opening a window and disabling the smoke detector dumped it into the same steel wastebasket he'd consigned Roger's file to, saturated it with charcoal starter and touched it off with a match. He used a long-handled steel spoon to stir the black and curling pages and switched on the fan in the hood above the range to draw the smoke out through the vent pipe. When the file was reduced to ashes, he carried the basket into the bathroom and flushed them down the toilet in relays to avoid clogging. If only bodies were as easily disposed of as the sum total of their occupants on paper.

"Jesus. Talk about your Viagra on wheels."

Roger's contact in the Detroit post of the

Michigan State Police had sent data to his onboard computer from the auto theft division, which allowed him to scroll through engineer's drawings and advertising illustrations of some eight hundred models of American-made muscle cars manufactured between 1960 and 1973.

Mustangs, GTOs, GTXs, Firebirds, Cobras, Cyclones, Galaxies, Road Runners, Dusters, Darts, Chargers, Challengers, Cougars; the names alone were composed to raise hard-ons. Blocks, hemis, spoilers, scoops; you needed a gearhead's glossary to follow the language.

He kept his hand on the clicker built into the dash and watched a dizzying parade of low-slung, attenuated silhouettes and exploded views of engines and drive trains flash across his screen. He'd had no idea how many different examples had been made available to a segment of the population that had grown weary of "your father's Oldsmobile," as one of the slogans ran in the ads his informant had included. It was a sub-culture he'd barely known existed, like book collecting and wine connoisseurship; and just as irrelevant.

It made him soporific, all those gaunt slanted images flashing like a sped-up chase scene in a cartoon, so that when the one he

154

was looking for came up he almost missed it, and had to scroll back to find it.

There it was: the 1970 Olds Cutlass, a two-door with an optional vinyl top and a 455-cubic-inch engine with standard two-barrel carburetor, four-barrel available on request. The fanciful painted glossy illustration exaggerated its earth-hugging proportions, making it longer than it appeared in photographs, and its finish looked as hard as porcelain and as deeply reflective as Crater Lake, bearing little resemblance to the faded chalky blue of the car he'd seen in Milford, the virginal white roof nothing like its dingy peeling example, but the sound its motor had made starting up was as clean and virile as the spotless chromed dynamo in the cutaway photo.

The restaurant lot was emptying, the dinner rush over. He got into line and called his man to report the identifying information.

"Okay, we've got a needle in a pile of needles instead of in a haystack," said the other. "Stick around."

"You stick around. You've got my cell. Start with cops. Retirees first. This one's a long way past his twenty."

"What makes him a cop?"

"He didn't get that limp sewing doilies."

155

"Man, I didn't sign on to do a fellow officer."

"You signed on. Wait, don't hang up."

He'd pulled back into Laurie Macklin's
street and slid into the curb a block down
from her building. A familiar vehicle was
parked in front of it.

"He's back," he said.

"Who's back?"

"Cutlass guy. Stand by for the plate number."

Me

Fifteen

She left the room without excusing herself. Since the pistol hadn't made a reappearance I took it she didn't expect to find me gone when she came back.

I killed time looking at prints on the walls. Her taste ran toward German expressionism: bright colors and jagged figures with exaggerated proportions set at precarious angles so that they looked as if they might fall out of the frames any second. It seemed an odd choice for a woman whose furnishings were quiet to the point of transparency; but it said a lot about her taste in husbands. A woman who lived not quite on the edge, but close enough to appreciate the view.

She came back wearing a pale yellow lambswool sweater with a boatneck that showed off her collarbone — a feature often overlooked by men who admire women — gray linen slacks with a crease, and gunmetal-colored slippers that left her ankles bare. Her hair was caught up by a dark blue figured bandanna tied at the nape of her neck, exposing a high forehead. The outfit came without pockets sufficient to conceal a firearm.

She saw me notice. "You might extend me the same courtesy."

I reached under my coattail, unclipped the .38, holster and all, and laid it on the apostrophe-shaped coffee table.

"I'm drinking," she said. "Gin and tonic. I have vodka, if you prefer."

"I don't. People who do don't drink for pleasure. Can I help?" There were no setups in the living room.

"I don't intend to poison you."

"Don't joke about that. Someone tried once."

Muscles pulled at the corners of her mouth. "I can't decide whether you've led an interesting life or you're a liar."

"A little of both. But I like to see how different people mix different drinks."

"For what it says about them?"

I grinned. The muscles at the corners of my mouth were looser than hers. "Every little movement has a meaning all its own."

Whoever had renovated the apartment had torn down most of the interior walls, leaving a clear expanse from the living room to the kitchen, small but arranged for efficiency: Ceramic floors, a freestanding stove with granite counters flanking the burners, a side-by-side refrigerator, open cupboards above a bright copper sink. She kept the liquor in a narrow cabinet with pull-out racks. A collection of footed glasses hung upside down from racks, like bats in an attic. It was Bombay Sapphire, a premium label. She filled two glasses a third of the way on one of the counters, topped them off from a bottle of Schweppes, and stirred them with a long-handled spoon. I accepted a glass, stroking the etched gold veins on the side with a thumb.

"Wedding present." She lifted her glass. "To Leroy."

"To his health?"

"In memoriam," she said, and drank.

"Sorry I missed him."

"You didn't miss much."

"How did he meet his end?"

"Someone blew him in half with a shotgun."

"Macklin?"

"Me."

I drank without mentioning the toast.

"His name was Landis," she said, "Roy, except most people called him Leroy, which was probably the real deal. He wanted me to call him Abilene. I called him Leroy."

"Uh-huh."

"Meaning?" A vertical line bifurcated her high brow.

"It's from the Latin for 'I'm listening, Mrs. Macklin. Or Ms. Ziegler; whatever.' "

The room was the living room: I had the wingback, she the sofa, same as before. Creatures in the animal kingdom pick their sites of advantage, creatures in the human kingdom too. We'd gone back to the Bombay for reinforcements, me mixing this time, two-to-one now. I felt a comfortable buzz, but if the gin had any effect on her, she was as good at concealing it as I was. How she'd learned at her tender age what it had taken me most of my career to develop may have had something to do with her marital situation; or maybe it came natural, like cloudy blue eyes.

"He came with a letter of introduction with Peter's signature, on our honeymoon in L.A. Peter'd been called away to supervise the sale of his camera business — I still thought he was in the camera business then — and Leroy was there to keep me company; take me to see the sights and whatever, so I wouldn't feel neglected. We took in the Chinese Theater and Tijuana. I had my picture taken standing next to one of those zebra-striped burros."

"Who wrote the letter?"

"I never found out. Leroy, probably. He was a tall drink of water, as I suppose they put it in Arkansas, where he said he was from. Fancied himself a cowboy, and dressed like it: Stetson hat, snap-front shirt, shit-kickers, the works. Mind if I use words like 'shit'?" She looked at me over her glass, holding it in both hands like the mug in her picture.

"I've got cable."

Her brow creased the other way, but she let it slide. "I was his hostage, was what I was. Bait. To lure Peter out into the open so Leroy could kill him."

"Wild guess," I said. "Leroy and Peter worked for the same firm till Peter gave notice. Only you don't quit that firm. It quits you."

"They'd tried before. I guess when I entered the picture they thought their luck had changed. Chink in the armor." She rolled a shoulder. "The boss's name was Major, Charles Major. Detroit man. Carlo Maggiore before he changed it. I got that much from Peter. That's when I found out he wasn't in the retail camera business."

"Maggiore. I heard that name."

163

"Not lately, unless you saw a rehash on *48 Hours* about mob history. He and Peter had butted heads before. Maggiore came off worse that time, so their differences were personal as well as professional. His luck didn't hold the second time. Somebody cut his throat in his own house in Beverly Hills — California, not Michigan. I can't say who, because I wasn't there. But I can guess. It wasn't long after Leroy —"

She drank. It was the first time she'd drawn on the gin as medicine. Until then we'd been two people drinking a hole in the early evening, like almost everyone else in the working world of metropolitan Detroit.

"It was in self-defense," she said. "Peter's, mine; makes no difference, he was going to kill one of us at least. It was in a car on the Pacific Coast Highway. Leroy had a knife, his weapon of choice. I had an antique shotgun, a joke meant to hang on a wall. I didn't even know if it would work.

"It did. Peter showed up — too late to do anything but help me with the burial at sea. Leroy." She drained the glass.

I toyed with mine. I don't drink to killers, dead or otherwise. "So why'd he bring it up? Macklin, I mean. To blackmail you into cooperating with me?"

"That's not Peter's — racket? Racket."

She drew a finger around the inside of her glass and licked it. "He'd be incriminating himself if he reported it. He told you to mention Leroy to remind me I'm no better than he is, that my life means more to me than someone else's. More than Leroy's, and more than Roger's. Well, he's right. I'd rather live. He just wanted to remind me of that, in case I got too proud to rely on help, considering the source."

"So am I hired?"

She blinked. "You still want the job?"

"Working for one killer against another killer? It's a new experience for sure."

"You left out one killer."

"You're not a killer, Mrs. Macklin."

"How can you say that?"

"Do you think we killers can't spot each other?"

She rolled her glass between her palms. "I think you should call me Laurie."

Sixteen

The apartment house was managed by a Realtor on the second floor of the old furniture store downtown. The receptionist wore ten yards of wool sweater with a snowman embroidered on it and silver hair in waves that brought a whole new meaning to the word *permanent*. A plastic replica of Santa and his reindeer took up most of a glitter mat on her desk. BAKER FIDELITY read a decal on the side of the sleigh. When I told the woman my business she leaned back in her swivel and shouted, "Ralph! Someone about Parkview!" That was the name of Laurie Macklin's apartment house.

A gargly male voice shouted back. She directed me through an open door. This was a big room, but there was barely space for a gargantuan old partners desk, an artificial Christmas tree, and a quartet of painted wooden nutcrackers three feet high. The man who got up to shake my hand might

166

have posed for the statues. His jowls hung loosely, making creases, so that his mouth looked as if it opened and shut on wooden hinges.

"Sorry I can't offer you a chair," he said. "I had to put it in storage. I let Nora go hog-wild with the decorations during the holidays." His gargle dropped to a whisper. "She lost her son in Desert Storm and she doesn't have any grandchildren."

I said that was okay — the chair thing, not the other — and gave him a card that carried only my name; to land offices in communities like that a private investigator is as ominous as a telegram from the War Department. It usually means the kind of scandal that had decided people to move out of the big city in the first place. He asked for references and I gave him Rosecranz in my office building. He pecked out the number on the phone on his desk, waited. "No one's answering."

The old Russian was probably out hunting cockroaches. I told Ralph to try Lauren Ziegler. "She's —"

He brightened at that and broke the connection. "I know Ms. Ziegler. The town's not that big." He dialed a number from memory and shot the breeze with the tenant while I admired his view of Milford. I was born in the same small town not too many miles from there, with the same stoplights that flashed yellow after ten o'clock and in December the same red-and-silver garlands on the streetlamps and lumps of frozen slush in the gutters. I'd spent the first ten years of my life clawing to get out and the rest of it clawing my way back.

But things are the same no matter the size of the city limits, or for that matter whether it's Kokomo or Katmandu: The kindly old gentleman who runs the hobby shop has images on his computer that could get him twenty years in stir, the devoted couple celebrate their golden anniversary with a butcher knife and a .44, the kid with the paper route throws in a Baggie filled with white powder for the house on the corner. Noxious weeds grow in all kinds of soil.

He hung up on a jovial note. "You're a friend, she says. That's fine. She always pays her rent on time and there have been no complaints from the other tenants." He drew a file from his deep drawer and opened it; frowned. "The attic room's available, but there's not much headroom."

I said I'd stoop.

"It's unfurnished."

"That's okay too." I kept a sleeping bag in the car for unexpected overnighters.

"Five hundred a month. We usually ask for first and last month up front, but since you're a friend of Miss Ziegler's —"

I got out my wallet and counted the bills onto the desk. He unlocked another drawer, put the money in a metal box, took out a ring of square brass keys with tags attached, separated one, and passed it across the desk. He wished me a merry Christmas and was humming the tune when I left.

Back in Detroit I broke open the purse again, but Chuck the urban explorer shook his head. It was almost dark in the empty building across from mine, but his dental work caught the light from the corner streetlamp. "You're good for all day, mister. You won't get that from the city."

"Much obliged. Find Tut's tomb yet?"

His grin broadened. "Nothing so spectacular, but a bro found a bottle of single-malt in an old piano last night in a warehouse."

"I wouldn't drink from it."

He touched my arm as I was leaving the old gas station. His voice dropped to a murmur. "You don't owe anybody money, do you?"

I followed the inclination of his head. The familiar Chevy was parked in a fifteen-minute loading zone half a block down from my building. "Just the county, the state, and Washington," I said. "These guys are with the city."

"Cops? They must want you bad. They've been there two hours. I was wondering why nobody came around to shoo 'em off."

Turning my back as a shield I smuggled a five-spot out of my wallet into a plaid flap pocket. "Got a phone?"

"Sure. Doesn't everyone?"

"Let me know if anything changes. My cell's on the back of my card."

"You in trouble?"

"I'm used to it, but you don't have to be. Keep the cash anyway."

"I didn't mean that. You're the first person hasn't told me to get a real job."

"I'd choke on it. I haven't had a real job since Saigon fell."

"What's that?"

"Theme park. Before your time."

The phone on the desk was ringing when I unlocked the private door. I scooped the mail off the floor inside the slot — it was all too brightly colored for checks or love letters — tipped it into the wastebasket in the kneehole, and picked up. The number on caller ID meant nothing; but most of my calls came from strangers. "A. Walker Investigations."

"Chuck, Mr. Walker. One of 'em's on his way up. He got out of the car as soon as you went inside."

I thanked him, scribbling his number on the pad. I'd never heard of urban explorers before that day, but you never know when you need one. I just got settled behind the desk when a shadow came to the pebbled glass.

"Come in, Officer," I said. "Or is it Sergeant?"

He had a heavy, handsome face with black brows, a prominent but not beaky nose, a wide mouth, and a raised white scar in a tiny ragged *C* on his blue chin just right of the cleft, likely left by a man's ring.

He was a big man; but they don't come in any other size in the department, in a knee-length camel's-hair coat over a navy suit and a trilby hat cocked at the right angle above his left eyebrow; gray necktie on a gray shirt. Threads of silver glittered at his temples.

"Detective." His voice was Tonto deep. "Stan Kopernick, First Grade. I told them that champagne color's too easy to spot."

"Shows how much I know. I thought it was brushed gold."

"There's the job to have. I guess if you said baby-shit yellow you wouldn't have it long." He stretched a hand the size of a La-

Z-Boy across the desk.

I took it, and here was one cop who didn't think he had to grind my bones to make his bread. There was power there, but held in reserve for when it counted.

"That was pretty slick there on seventy-five," he said, planting himself in the customer's chair. "Reed's not easy to lose."

"Reed should know better than to try not to be lost."

"Where'd you go?"

"That would defeat the purpose, Detective."

He patted the camel's-hair. "I never leave the office without grabbing a fistful of John Does. Obstructing justice, that's a Swiss Army knife in my trade."

"You'd have to serve one to every driver that got between you and me on the interstate. There's nothing on the statutes that says a man can't go motoring in the afternoon. In this town it's practically a requirement."

"I don't want to get tough."

"I know. You just can't help it. Does Lieutenant Stonesmith know you came up here to brace me, or was that your own brainstorm?"

"She didn't say one way or the other, but I'd probably do what I wanted to anyway. I don't take orders so good from a woman." He leaned forward, resting his forearms on the desk. "I work out of the old Third, Walker. That mean anything to you?"

"I thought I knew everyone in Homicide."

"I'm just back from the minors. They sent me down for retraining after the Gang Squad broke up."

"Everyone thought you boys went away after that. They just threw you back into the mixing bowl and poured you out in little cups, same as STRESS and the old Racket Squad. No sense wasting all that street savvy."

"MBA, we call it: Maul, Batter, and Assault, all in the interest of maintaining the peace."

"How long have you been trying to sprinkle salt on Peter Macklin's tail?"

His hat rode up his forehead. "Who said anything about him?"

"No one had to. Nothing ever changes in the department except the look. A ladies' room installed in Thirteen Hundred, no third-degree in the basement, nothing so obvious, not so many flashlights built like blackjacks, good fitness program in place to keep the bellies from hanging over the gun belts, cameras on lapels, everything modern in all the areas visible to the public, but it's all the same at the core. The cops operate the way they did at the start: all the warlords marking their territories, like dogs."

"Not such a bad system. What good's having separate details, you don't honor them? When did Murder One stop being a major crime? Who invited Diana Ross anyway?"

The question wasn't racist or sexist on the face of it: An HR committee could dismantle it, inspect all the parts, and put it back together without reaching a conclusion. If sensitivity training had had any visible effect on haters, it was in the way the professionals chose their weapons.

"I don't know where Macklin is, Kopernick. If that's why you tied a firecracker to my tail, you wasted a match."

"Peter Macklin? He's one for the cold-case crowd. It's fresh meat I'm after. It's his boy Roger I want."

I let that one slide off my poker face. I'd only stopped by the office to look at the mail and check for messages; I clean forgot Stonesmith's centurions would have gone back there as a default line after I dumped them. I needed to set up shop in Milford, but if I brought a train with me they'd put things together and book her as a material witness for her own safety. That would be chicken soup for Roger's soul. Suspicious suicide was no stranger to the Wayne County Jail.

Kopernick got tired of waiting for me to respond. "Roger's still a kid. He gives up his contacts, his old man included, he's out in ten with some lead still in his pencil. I didn't make plainclothes throwing myself up against the thickest part of the wall."

Just then something hummed. He shifted positions, pulled a phone the size of motel soap out of his coat and muttered into it. He listened, said, "Okie-doke," and put it away. He stood. "Mama spank. She radioed Reed. We're not supposed to make contact."

"One of those orders I guess you don't take from women," I said.

His baggy grin had come with the shield. "We all got to get used to shit. I've killed six men and one woman, defending myself and on the run. That was back in the day. If you were dumb enough to say you didn't shoot to kill, you got suspended. Now, not so much. You don't adjust to the situation, they throw you a party and give you the boot. So that's my advice: Adjust to the situation. We don't shake so easy the second time."

I waited until the hall door banged shut, got up and checked the waiting room and the landing just to be sure, and called the number that had popped up on my caller ID. When Dr. Chuck came on his cell, I asked him if a quick twenty would help him explore the city. I got the answer I expected and told him where he could find the hideout key to the car.

Ten minutes later I stood at the window, watching around the edge of the blind at the street below. The Cutlass slid out the open bay of the deserted building and turned southeast toward downtown. Kopernick and his partner hadn't seen me come out of the building, so there was a little hesitation before the Chevy swung behind, its tires chirping on the U-turn. When I was sure they'd swallowed the bait I called a cab and went home to pack.

SEVENTEEN

"How do you know how much you'll need?"

He was sitting in my best chair when I came out of the bedroom carrying a suitcase. I noticed then he didn't cross his legs, seated on the edge of the cushion with his feet flat on the floor and his hands spread palms down on the arms. I couldn't tell if he was armed; his leather windbreaker was built for a heftier man. He would buy most of his jackets that way, to accommodate the extra load.

I flung the case onto the swayback sofa, going for my belt in the same movement. He held his position. The revolver in my hand might as well have been a toothbrush.

"I didn't get around to fixing that garage window," I said.

"It wouldn't matter if you had. You know what they say about locks."

I returned the .38 to its clip. "I always pack for a week. Most of the work I get doesn't take any longer than that. If it does, there are Laundromats. I can't remember the last time a case took me to the Gobi."

Peter Macklin tilted a hand toward a manila folder on my coffee table. "You move fast for someone who's collected so many aches and pains. I'm not just talking about GSW. I've got a couple of those myself."

"Okay if I take a look? I'm past due for a checkup."

He said nothing. I scooped up the folder and paged through my medical file. "You left out the patient privacy information."

"That's to keep honest people out. Like locks. What I can't figure out is why you don't stutter."

"I'm guessing you went through my medicine cabinet."

"I was pretty sure I wouldn't find anything stronger than over-the-counter. I can usually spot it when someone's still using."

"If you're talking about concussions, I've had a lot of experience in picking myself up off strange floors. But I can still dress myself and work crossword puzzles, if the words aren't too big. I took an aptitude test when I got out of the service. It called for a thick skull. That didn't leave much room for brains; but what are those in detective work?" I flung myself next to the suitcase and shook loose a cigarette. "You're wasting your time on me when you should be reading about Roger."

"There wasn't as much to read; but you're wasting time I need. Roger's my lookout, not yours. I hired you to protect my wife."

I lit up. "I thought I felt someone watching me. I thought it was the usual small-town snoop, or cops, which I handle on a case-by-case basis; but I'm the careful type, so I checked it out. Roger take a size ten shoe?"

"Nine and a half. There's always some distortion in snow and frost. I could have told you where that last picture was taken from. Things are going to take twice as long if you're going to cover the same ground I already did."

"I could say the same thing about you."

"Casing's like carpentry: Measure twice, cut once."

"So is sleuthing. It's part of the work, checking up on the story you get from the client. For all I knew, you took those pictures yourself. It wouldn't be the first time someone hired me to draw attention away from him."

"I take an eight. He got his feet from his mother's side." He drew a breath, purely in the interest of feeding his lungs. "I still feel

179

about Laurie the way I always did. Roger knows that. He spelled it out in his email." He lifted the same hand. "Keep the file. I can always get more."

"Meaning you can always get *me.*"

"I'm like you. I work the job."

I was beginning to enjoy the conversation, if not the company. I had no idea why.

"What are you going to do when Dorfman's gone?" I said. "These days it's a lot harder digging up confidential information from scratch."

"Dorfman's not going anywhere. Lawyers are tough to kill, and crooked ones never die. They just keep playing the angles until they run out of them; and they never run out of angles. What did Laurie say when you brought up Leroy?"

"How do you know I had to?" I blew smoke at the ceiling. "Forget it. She told me she killed him and you helped her dump the body in the ocean. Was that on the level, or did you do it and let her think it was her?"

"Why would I do that?"

"To bind her tight. To make her think she's as bad as you."

"Is bad important to you?"

"If you have to ask that question, you just answered mine."

"Your world's that simple, good and evil?"

"That simple, if you look at the situation long enough."

"No gray areas?"

"People talk about them. When they do I know what side they're on."

"I can't figure out whether you're naïve or a cockeyed idealist."

"I'm okay with both. Did you kill Leroy and let Laurie think it was her?"

"She told you the circumstances?"

"She said it was self-defense. He had a knife, she had a shotgun no one could be sure would work. I thought that was a nice touch. It leveled the playing field."

"It didn't. He was an experienced killer, a psychopath. It could easily have gone the other way. Civilians hesitate. He underestimated her. That's all she had."

"That and the shotgun."

"This is hearsay. I'm telling you what she told me."

"I asked her if your bringing up Leroy was some kind of blackmail, to get her to agree to our arrangement. She said it was to remind her you're not the only killer in the marriage."

"I doubt she meant that. You're a stranger. She's learned to be suspicious of people she doesn't know. It was my way of telling her you're acting for me. She and I were the only ones who knew about Leroy. Even the man who sent him thought I was the one who made him disappear. Either I hired you for the reason I gave or to set her up, in which case I wouldn't have sent her that message. You can't have it both ways."

The cigarette had gone bitter. I ditched it in a tray. "You called Leroy a psychopath. What makes you different?"

"He killed because he liked it."

"You don't?"

"Do you like detective work?"

"I did at the start. So it's just a job to you."

"I turn down work I don't like. We have that in common."

I said, "I'd retire tomorrow if I had the money. If Roger thinks he can tap you for a hundred grand, it means you've got more, probably a lot more. Why are you still working?"

"Who said I am?"

"Don't try to sell me Roger doesn't count because no one's paying you to kill him. He's giving you an out. You can pay him off and walk away clean. Whatever's between you, you're still blood."

He was standing now, looking down at me with his hands hanging at his sides. We'd met only twice, but I'd figured out they were always empty in company except when

182

he was holding a weapon.

"You're smarter than that. You forget I checked up on you. It's not money he wants, or Laurie's life. Neither one is enough. He wants me to give in, and then he's going to kill her with me watching, then kill me — if he can — or hang her murder on me just for garnish. That doesn't come from my side of the family, or his mother's. He's a self-made man."

He reached behind him; I jumped for the .38. He saw the movement. As far as he was concerned I was checking my watch for the time. From a hip pocket he drew a fold of currency and tossed it on the coffee table.

I said, "You paid me, remember?"

"There's two thousand there. Fifteen hundred won't get you far. If Roger was watching the apartment while you were inside it, he knows by now who you are, and can guess why. Leaving you as a witness would upset all his plans."

"I'm not a witness till he follows through. I'd've thought you had more faith in yourself than that."

"I might miss," he said. "It's happened before."

Eighteen

"Cozy. Reminds me of the night I spent in an airport waiting room when all the runways were socked in."

I stood next to Laurie Macklin in the doorway, reviewing my pied-à-terre for an indefinite period. I'd spread my sleeping bag on squares of peel-and-stick linoleum and under it chipboard, stacked some books next to it and tins of deviled ham, canned tuna, and baby potatoes on the exposed two-by-fours that kept the sloped roof from collapsing like a fort made of sofa cushions; four plastic jugs of drinking water on the floor. A faux Tiffany lamp that had been rescued from above someone's pool table hung from a stiff cord above the sleeping bag. Someone had installed a two-burner electric range, a microwave oven big enough to heat up one bagel at a time, and a toilet and triangular sink enclosed in a hinged screen that belonged to the Ikea dynasty.

Some kind of light, from the moon or a streetlamp, filtered in through a window wedged in the triangle of the north wall.

It wasn't a hovel, unless that was what you wanted. Add chairs, a sofa, tables, a proper bed, bookshelves, bright wallpaper, curtains, some wall art, and *Architectural Digest* wouldn't exactly sniff at it. But if you wanted a place to be temporary, I'd taken all the right steps. This wasn't home. It was a hunting camp, to be exited as soon as I'd taken my trophy.

Which was Laurie Macklin, in the condition in which I'd found her. The room was directly above hers. A brace-and-bit might have come in handy, to drill a hole in the floor; but as it was I could hear most of what went on below. She'd been watching the Food Network, and the soufflé recipe had come through clear enough to try it for myself, if I knew how to crack an egg.

"I had a better billet in Cambodia," I said, "in a bamboo hut, including an eight-hundred-dollar Japanese stereo system I bought for sixty bucks from a tunnel rat. But of course there was a war going on."

"How'd you know how much to pack?"

"Your husband asked me the same question; but he was just making conversation."

She turned toward me. She had on the

sweater and slacks she'd changed into from her robe a couple of hours earlier. The varicolored light from the glass-shaded lamp found tiny fissures in the corners of her eyes. It was one of those flaws I look for in women. When I couldn't find them, I wondered how much money had gone into getting rid of them and where it had come from.

"You saw him since we met?" she said.

"He invited himself into my house. He has a habit of doing that, whether I'm there or not. I can keep mice out but not him."

"I don't suppose he mentioned me."

"Mrs. Macklin, you're the only person he talks about except his son."

She hugged herself. The room was a little chilly at that, heated by only a square register in an aluminum duct running up the wall opposite the door. "Fathers and sons. What is it about them, and why can't they get along?"

"The Greeks had a theory. Then too there's the you-broke-my-mother thing."

"I never met Roger. I wanted to go to Donna's funeral, but Peter said no. He was right, I guess. It would be like inviting her to our wedding."

"Just as well you didn't hook up. No one should know more than one killer, even socially."

"By that I take it to mean you've known more than your share."

"I'm not sure they hand out shares. If they do, I guess I'd have the corner. Most killers turn out to be a disappointment; like when you meet a celebrity you've heard about all your life. The conversation's limited. Anyone can be famous, and killing's a snap. Ask any goldfish."

"Why do you do what you do?"

"Why did you marry Macklin?"

"I probably wouldn't have, if I'd known what he was."

"If I'd known what the work's like, I'd have become a telephone lineman. I'd be just as obsolete now, but I'd probably have all my teeth."

"If you didn't slip."

"Still better than killers."

"So what's the procedure? Do I bang on my ceiling with a broom handle when I'm in distress? Maybe in some kind of code, so if it's just one of my neighbors complaining about a loud TV you can roll over and go back to sleep?"

"A scream should do it. I'll probably hear anything unusual. The house is solid, but they saved a bunch of bucks when they finished the attic." I stamped a heel on the ply. "I could pretty much map your movements when I was up here unpacking. You flushed the toilet twice — ran water in the sink both times, I'm happy to say — opened the refrigerator once, poured something fizzy into what was probably a tall glass, from the time it took, clunked in two ice cubes, and surfed through about seventeen channels before you found one worth looking at; only you switched off just when the hostess turned on the oven."

"I can't say I'm happy about that — not the cooking lesson, just a stranger knowing I don't cook and that I wash my hands after I pee."

"Don't worry about me. I'm the place where secrets go to die."

"I only heard a board or two creak up here."

"That's as much as you can expect to hear when Walker's on the job. Stealthy is my middle name."

"You don't have a middle name. I looked up your investigator's license on the Lansing site."

"I can't say I'm happy about that — not the no-middle-name thing. Nobody uses them except angry mothers. I don't care for strangers knowing I don't have one."

"I can keep a secret same as you. So do I

entertain you or what? I'm new to this bodyguard business."

"You can make up your own rules. The protocol's all on my side. If you're still alive when I punch out, I came through on it. You don't even have to know I'm in the same Zip code. I should warn you: Bodyguards have a nasty habit of shooting last."

"Encouraging."

"It gets worse. Some people think it was a Secret Service slug that killed JFK. He got caught in the crossfire."

"Everybody killed JFK. Frankly, I felt safer when I was with Peter."

"You were, but I can't get that close."

She turned my way, and the murky blue eyes took on a new layer of haze. "If that's your idea of seduction, you're rusty."

"I had those kinds of ideas yanked out with my wisdom teeth, Mrs. Macklin. Call my cell when you're planning to leave the house. I'll try to stay out of your hip pockets even then."

My supper was deviled ham, eaten straight from the can with a spoon, with a mineral water chaser; I'd been in too much of a hurry to get to the apartment after the Peter Macklin delay at home to stop for bread. The attic room hadn't been advertised as nonsmoking, but there was a smoke detector screwed to a rafter. I dismantled it, letting its innards dangle, cracked the window in the north wall, and smoked until I got sleepy, stretched out in the sleeping bag unzipped all the way in case I had to break out of the chrysalis in a hurry, with the Chief's Special in easy reach on the floor.

I put out the cigarette and drifted off to the soothing strains of *The Golden Girls* chirruping up through the floor from the apartment below; every minute of every day an episode is playing somewhere. I doubted Mrs. Macklin was a fan, but the prattle of mature women wrestling with post-menopausal sex is like white noise for the troubled; and one-half of a couple going through the clinical practice of separating for life was trouble enough, without the killing-threat thing.

That was just projection, maybe. For all I knew, the Ohio farm girl who'd married a Detroit killer-for-hire (I'd looked her up, too, through an acquaintance with twenty-first-century connections) was having the time of her life breaking all bonds to the underside of existence as we know it and exploring the world on top. She was on the left side of thirty, after all, with two-thirds of her life left to play out.

But you don't get those cloudy eyes in the maternity ward. Those you had to earn.

NINETEEN

This one was a challenge.

Any naturalist prepared himself for it, the creature in captivity behaving entirely differently from its life in the wild. It knows it's being watched, and so behaves as expected and by constriction, rather than by natural instinct.

It shouldn't have meant anything to me. I was there to keep the creature alive, not study and record its habits; but one needs his diversions.

Laurie Macklin took phone calls from friends and professional contacts — she was a travel agent, it turned out; a calling as obsolete as my own in the world of instant information. But it provided her with the means to work at home by computer. Her special talent, from what drifted my way from this end of the conversations, was comparing rates among airlines, cruise companies, and hotels and playing them off against each other, playing every card from AARP to military service and hardship cases, and in the last ditch dialing up the feminine charm. Add-on charges collapsed when her tone got throaty, amenities increased, and at least one desk clerk asked to take her to dinner — the early-bird seating, which when translated meant a wife at home.

When the voice came out, a combination of early Kathleen Turner and late Jean Harlow, it meant she'd grown accustomed to the situation, if she hadn't actually forgotten about it. The breakthrough came halfway through my third day in the bell tower. I wasn't sure I'd heard it at first, so I cranked down the thermostat to increase concentration. When the blower fan mounted inside the heating duct switched off, the register worked like a baby monitor. I could get used to listening to that voice.

By then we'd been outside a few times, once to stretch our legs around the little park, another to buy fresh produce from the little chain supermarket four blocks away, again to eat lunch in a restaurant that served a dozen tables in a Wilson-era farmhouse with a wraparound porch for open-air dining in warm weather.

We ate at separate tables; but we found

each other at liberty outside, where I offered to escort her home.

"We're not fooling anyone," she said, as
we set out.

"I'd be disappointed in Roger, if we were,"
I said. "I'm going into Detroit tomorrow.
It'd be more convenient all around if you'd
accompany me."

"That would depend on the destination."

"It's romantic as all hell, if you're drawn
to the library on Woodward. I'm interested
in what the papers had to say about how
Charles Major met his end. Indulge me," I
said. "You can treat yourself to lunch in
Greektown. We'll charge the bill to your
soon-to-be-ex-husband. If he killed Major, I
need to know. Investigating the client's as
important as the investigation he hired you
to do."

She turned to face me. The weird warm
spell was still in force; she wore a fall jacket
I'd seen before, in a photograph, and a
stretchy ear-muffler, which she'd loosened
to let fall around her neck because the air
wasn't cold enough to pink her lobes.
"Tomorrow's Sunday."

"By golly, so it is. We can stop by a church
if that's what you want."

"I'm as bookish as the next girl, if the next
girl isn't Evelyn Wood; but I don't intend to

spend any part of my weekend in a dusty old library."

"It's not so dusty. You can eat off the floor in the microfilm reading room. You can ask any of the tramps who sleep there."

"Nobody eats off the floor in my apartment. But I've got a gizmo in it that can track down anything you could find on microfilm, without the ninety-minute drive round-trip."

"Maybe I'm homesick."

"I'm your responsibility, Mr. Walker, not your prisoner. It's my place or nothing."

"Laurie, that's just about the sexiest ultimatum I've ever had."

"If that's what you think it is, you need to go back to calling me Mrs. Macklin."

She'd set up her office in a corner of her bedroom, a pale blue room with strong light streaming in through the west windows. A printed spread covered the bed, and for once in the history of women living alone it wasn't heaped with pillows and cushions. There was an antique curve-front bureau painted soft white, with a mirror, a slipper chair upholstered in yellow silk or rayon, and a laptop sitting closed on a vanity table painted to match the bureau but no vanity items visible. It was one of those heartbreaking winter days with no snow clouds in sight; the sky was bright enamel and it hurt to look at it. She drew the curtains, but there was still no need to turn on a light.

I drew the slipper chair up alongside her swivel, perched on the edge, and watched her flip up the screen and power up.

"You really don't use one of these?" she said, stroking the built-in mouse.

"I know who to go to when I need it. Apart from that the work's the same as at the start, gasoline and shoe leather and sometimes brains. Try the *News* first."

"Major was killed in California."

"He made his bones in Detroit. The locals keep tabs on all the hometown boys and when it comes to crime reporting they can't be beat. They've had more practice than most."

"It wasn't long after — after Leroy." Her fingers hopscotched across the keyboard. When the website came up, a hodgepodge of twenty-first-century graphics and the paper's Ye Olde masthead, she found a legend, scrolled, chose a file, scrolled and scrolled; the principle was the same as cranking the mechanical microfilm readers at the library, only the images flashed by faster, like subliminal messages aimed at a focus group.

I watched, but I gave no directions. I had a vague idea of what Carlo Maggiore/ Charles Major would look like; mob bosses tend to run to patterns established by Hollywood. For the old-timers it was James Cagney and George Raft, for their successors Robert De Niro in *Goodfellas,* Al Pacino in both *Godfathers,* Al Pacino in *Scarface,* Al Pacino in *Carlito's Way.* Slick hair, good tailors, and the kind of practiced swagger that shows even when they're standing still. What they did before the studios came along to show them how to walk and talk and blow their nose I couldn't guess.

When she came to a stop on a front page picture, I realized my list was incomplete.

It was a walking shot, taken with a long lens on some anonymous street, then blown up and cropped to serve as a trunk photo: A middle-aged character in three-quarter profile with the collar of a sports shirt rolled out over his lapels, a tiny gold hoop in his ear, and the obligatory dark glasses straddling a thick nose curdled like porridge. His fair hair was rumpled, needed trimming, and he listed toward a deformed left shoulder which some expert padding in the right couldn't quite balance out. The man was a hunchback. The two-column headline ran:

ALLEGED LOCAL CRIME CHIEF
MURDERED IN CALIFORNIA

In the old days, the byline would have been Barry Stackpole's, my go-to source whenever organized crime reared its pug-ugly head; he'd had a lock on the paper's investigative beat for years. But he'd long since drifted on to a local TV show, then a column on the internet, and currently a streaming program posting mugs of under-world figures, regular updates on their activities, and the names of certain every-day products and services whose profits financed traffic in drugs, weapons, human organs, and slave labor.

His successor, a woman whose name I didn't recognize, seemed professional enough, avoiding speculation and attribut-ing official reports. Major, a second-generation American who by all accounts had performed his last legal act when he'd changed his name, had been alone in his Beverly Hills home watching TV when someone crept up behind him and cut his throat. He'd died within minutes.

There followed a roster of his active interests in labor racketeering, narcotics smuggling, loan-sharking, gambling, fenc-ing stolen property, and questioning by authorities in Michigan and California in connection with several homicides, but attempts to indict him for violating the Racketeer Influenced and Corrupt Organizations Act (RICO) had failed for lack of evidence, although several witnesses had come forward, and moved backward in short order, including two who'd backed off the edge of the earth. The L.A.P.D. spokesman was of the opinion that Major had been targeted by rivals for his position in the rackets.

"That's always the fallback," I said. "I wonder if both those no-shows were Macklin's work too."

"We don't even know if Major was. But Leroy said he was working for him, and even I know the best way to prevent anyone from taking Leroy's place is to remove the man who paid his way. Peter isn't a man to overlook things. Should we keep searching?"

"They'd just be rehashing, trying to keep the story alive until the punchline. Which in these cases almost never comes about, and didn't this time, if we're right and it was Macklin. I think we're right." I sat back. "Thanks. I like to know everything I can about who's paying *my* way."

"Would that change anything?"

"Not if he's on the up-and-up."

She turned her head. The look on her face

made me laugh.

"Up-and-up as to the job," I said. "If I come through as arranged and he doesn't terminate my services the way he did his employment with Major." I looked again at the dead man. "Deb Stonesmith said Macklin's as good with an edged weapon as he is with a gun. At the time I thought she was exaggerating for effect."

She shut the lid of the laptop and we went back into the living room.

"Now that we've lined our stomachs with food, shall we move on to the drinking part of the day?" She started toward the kitchen.

"Just one for me."

"Of course. Keep your wits —"

She was crossing in front of the living room window, with me following. Just then I got one of those chills you get. I threw my arms around her and flung myself sideways, taking her with me. We hit the floor hard, but I hardly felt the impact. The window coming apart distracted me.

■ ■ ■ ■

HER

■ ■ ■ ■

TWENTY

"Get the fucking sweater! Jesus Christ! Button it up to your ears. You get hot, you can take off your goddamn panties."

Wanting her sweater had been just an excuse. The wind blowing across the Pacific Coast Highway was damp with the ocean, but she wasn't really cold, and hadn't been when she'd thrown it in the backseat. She'd just done that to cover what was lying across it.

It was a rented Buick, and just then it seemed the only safe place in the world; certainly not out here in the open, with no one to see the lanky lantern-jawed drugstore cowboy with his oversize folding knife. He practically shoved her toward the car, and she used the momentum to tear open the door against the powerful gust from the ocean walloping the shore, drowning out whatever obscenities he was still screaming at her. He'd said he was taking her back to his place in West Hollywood until Peter came looking for her; but she'd spent enough time in the man's company — was it really less than a week? — it seemed like months since she'd been on her — honeymoon. She threw herself headlong across the seat, her hands on the sweater and the hard angular thing underneath. From some instinct, Leroy snatched hold of the door for leverage and lunged, the broad blade he'd been sharpening and oiling since he'd bought it in the sporting goods department at Kmart catching the light of the dying sun, sparking a memory; she was brought up on a farm and had seen hogs stuck in the neck at slaughtering time, the neon-bright arc their blood made gushing from the artery, that same impossibly hot shade of orange.

She managed to twist herself around just as his weight was pressing her onto her face. There was no time to release the shotgun from its pink shroud. It was an old-fashioned one with side-by-side barrels like Elmer Fudd carried "hunting wabbits." She swung the barrels until something dense stopped them and jerked both triggers. The roar boxed her ears. Bits of pink fluff swirled like glitter in a shaken snow globe, her nostrils shrank from the stench of scorched wool, burnt powder, and cooked flesh, the last like roast pork . . .

And when she recovered enough from the

shock of all those senses going off at once, only sight and smell remained, because she was deaf now to the pounding of the surf (and would have a ringing in her ears long after hearing returned), and even the pain of trying to fill paralyzed lungs hadn't yet registered itself. In the presence of a man who'd been torn in half by a double load of ten-gauge buckshot in the belly, pain had no meaning. In time she'd be grateful for it, because that was a privilege Leroy wouldn't know again.

All of this played in her head as she said simply, "I had an antique shotgun. I didn't even know if it would work.

"It did. . . ."

Laurie studied the detective's face for his reaction, but it revealed no more than Peter's had when she'd confronted him with what he did for a living. Were the men who followed such work born that way, she wondered, did they develop it, or did it come along on its own, like learning to tell if an ear of corn is ripe before you tear open the husk, exposing it to ruin? This face was different physically, older but far from worn, had been handsome and was still striking, set solidly on square shoulders with obvious strength in the muscles of the neck. Other things differed more significantly. The eyes were a greenish shade of brown and almost gentle looking, but sad, with a haze of pain that struck her as chronic. As he'd listened, the deep lines bracketing his mouth tightened until they were almost invisible.

"I don't drink to killers," he said, when she raised a glass to Leroy.

She'd called herself a killer, and Walker had said something to the effect that one swallow doesn't make a summer, hinting that he was no stranger to slaughter himself.

She agreed to let him look after her, if he could find accommodations. "I've lived with someone all my life," she said. "I moved in with Peter straight from my parents' house in Ohio. I'm still getting used to keeping my own company. I don't intend to start over from scratch again. It would be like going backward."

"That suits me. I like to leave the seat up."

She promised not to go out until he came back, although she was probably safe enough until either Roger had an answer to his demand or Macklin paid him — which wasn't going to happen, they agreed. An hour and a half later he knocked on her door again to say he'd moved in directly over her head.

"I was watching through the window," she said. "I didn't see anyone drive up."

"I had a cab drop me off three blocks over

and walked in across lots. I heard from a friend on the way here. His name's Chuck. He's taking the grand tour of the northwestern suburbs at the wheel of my car with a police escort close behind. It probably won't surprise you your husband's popular with the authorities. Me, too, by association."

She nodded. "I've met Lieutenant Stonesmith. I liked her, but I'm not expecting a Christmas card."

"Don't count on that. Cops live in a Bizarro world. Upright citizens who crack too easy make them nervous. Care to see the new digs? I'm not Martha Stewart, but I know chintz don't go with paisley."

She was just starting to get comfortable with him, preceding him toward the kitchen bar, when her arms were pinned to her sides and she slammed on her side on the floor. It was as sudden as slipping on an unexpected patch of ice; one instant vertical, the next horizontal, gasping to fill her lungs with enough air to cry out. She was back in her rent-a-car outside Montecito, struggling to free herself from Leroy's wiry grasp. It hadn't been just the pounding of the waves she'd heard, she knew now, but her pulse hammering between her temples. She'd fallen for it a second time: a friendly stranger sent by Peter to keep her company, but who'd been sent by someone else whose motives were more sinister. She'd learned nothing from experience, and there would be no more opportunities to get wise. Cause of death? Trust in the common decency of man.

Then the room filled with a noise louder than her heartbeat, as loud as the shotgun report, and pieces of something showered her, pattering against her sweater like hail. One of them stung her behind the ear, something trickled down her neck, and it was no hail, it was glass. She stopped struggling, but the weight continued to hold her down, the arms encircling her as taut as thick hawser. She felt his warm breath in her ear, just ahead of where she was bleeding. It smelled of coffee. He must have stopped for a cup on his way to Detroit, to cut the effect of the gin he'd drunk on his last visit.

Leroy wouldn't have done that. His type wasn't that kind of cautious. Peter wouldn't have drunk at all — or eaten, for that matter, until the crisis was in remission. This man Walker was a similar species of creature to them both, yet not the same; a puzzle.

"Are you hit?"

Of course he'd seen the blood. He lifted

himself far enough for her to free a hand. It came back from behind her ear with a smear, no more.

She resisted the urge to pat herself all over, like a slapstick comic. "It was the glass, I think. Is it bad?" The throbbing had begun.

He took her chin in one hand, turned her head. "I've done worse shaving." Clothing rustled. Something crisp and smelling of starch pressed itself to the nick. What man carries a handkerchief these days?

He shifted his weight more, giving her complete movement. Shards of glass shifted, slid, and landed on the floor with an almost merry tinkle, like icicles falling from a roof. She took over the operation, sitting up on one hip with the fold of cloth pressed to her neck. He was bleeding too, she saw then, a scarlet rivulet meandering from just beneath his right eye all the way down his neck and staining the collar of his white shirt. The shower of glass had caught him before he could turn his own face away.

"You need this more than I do." She folded her own blood inside the handkerchief and pressed it to his cheek. He let her dab at it, then took charge. Looked at the cloth. "Nothing for the diary here. It's just my second scratch since Thanksgiving."

"You've done worse shaving, I know."

"Worse yet. I've got a tab at Detroit Receiving. Two more visits and the next one's free. A little iodine wouldn't hurt either of us. Well, just a sting."

"Who has iodine? You can *joke* about this?" Her voice shook. The shock was setting in.

"Take a deep breath, then take another. I joke so I don't have to."

She inhaled, exhaled. Again.

He studied her. "Air tastes sweet, doesn't it?"

"I don't want it to taste sweet. I want it to taste like air."

The world these people lived in wasn't hers. If she'd had any second thoughts about divorce, she didn't have them now. Every mile she put between herself and Macklin and Walker and all their sort was a mile to the good.

The detective twisted onto his own hip, and she saw he was holding a handgun, a revolver with a rubber grip and a short barrel. It seemed a cap pistol compared to most of the ones that floated around Peter's world, heavy weapons with huge muzzles, although the overall shape was similar to the kind Peter armed himself with, when he armed himself; squat things built of separate components that could be broken down and put back together swiftly, like Legos. Peter was a different man once he'd ridden himself of one. The man she'd married.

"Was it a gunshot?" she said. "I know that sounds stupid. I keep hoping it was a juvenile delinquent with a rock."

"Me, too. Where's a juvie when you need one? It was a rifle, if I'm right about the distance; we'll go into that later if you want. Not fired from the gazebo, not in broad daylight. There are some commercial buildings on the other side of the park, with flat roofs and no guards to keep people from using them. Why should there be, in Milford? Just one shot and then he'd be gone before anyone got around to tracing it to the source."

She shook herself loose of the image. "I thought you said I'd be okay until Roger heard back from Peter. Do you think he has?"

"Macklin would've let us know; otherwise why hire me?"

"A warning?"

"Maybe; but not for you. Macklin said Roger was his lookout, not mine. That's changed."

TWENTY-ONE

"What do I do now?" she asked.

Walker said, "What do honest people do? Call nine-one-one. Just say someone broke your window. Don't give them any more information over the phone except your name and address."

She was dialing when they heard a siren.

He took away the receiver and cradled it. "I forgot. This isn't Detroit. The neighbors here report this kind of thing. It's better to leave it to them while you see to that cut. That's what honest people do. Can you manage it?"

"The cut? Oh, please."

"The whole thing."

"You talked to Deborah Stonesmith. What do you think?"

"That's what I meant. You were cool with her because you had to be. Here, cool's bad. Your window exploded and a piece of glass cut you. You've got the jitters."

"I do, actually."

"Good. Turn them loose for the cops." He went toward the door.

"You won't be here?"

"I never was. You don't want to explain why you were entertaining a plastic badge when someone busted your window."

"What do I say?"

"You were heading for the kitchen and, crash!"

"What if they ask if I'm married?"

"You're single, Miss Ziegler. Don't volunteer anything. They may ask if you live alone, no more, and maybe not even that. Every day someone somewhere is shot at, and most of the time it's at random. Not so often in places like Milford, but it happens. All you're leaving out is a domestic mess that's nobody else's business and that you're being protected by a hired hand. You don't know why what happened happened. You don't, you know. You don't even know what broke your window. Remember that. If you say it was a shot, they'll want to know how you know. Even I didn't hear the report, and I'm supposed to notice such things."

"Can't I just tell them I found the bullet in the wall?"

Which they had. He'd paced a straight line to the wall opposite and found the blemish in the plaster.

"You're a civilian. You're too dumb to think about looking for such things. Doesn't matter that anyone who's ever watched television knows how cops work. They like to think they're exclusive."

"Okay." The siren was getting closer.

"I'll come back when the coast is clear. Remember, tell them everything about the window, except without me, and you don't know anything about a shot."

He left. She'd just finished cleaning and disinfecting the nick behind her ear and sticking on a Band-Aid when the siren wound down in front of the building.

The officer who did most of the talking, pudgy, with a brush moustache and a spray of dandruff on his epaulets, took her identification and recorded the information in a notebook, the dime-store kind with a spiral at the top. His partner said little and did less. He was younger than she was. She'd been told that would happen someday.

The older man was less perfunctory than the police in Detroit; he seemed genuinely concerned that a local citizen had been put in danger. He asked to see her injury and she turned her head and pushed her hair away from the Band-Aid.

"Are you sure you don't need stitches?"

She shook her head. "I was brought up in the country. I know how to deal with scrapes and bruises."

She answered all his questions in the same tone, the lies as well as the truth:

No, sir, I have no enemies that I know of.

Yes, I live alone.

I've lived here almost six weeks.

No special reason, except I got tired of Southfield. I told you, I'm a country girl.

He asked more questions while the partner roamed the living room, being careful to avoid stepping on broken glass.

"Gordy."

He was standing by the wall opposite the window. His partner joined him, peered at the hole, raised a hand and bored a finger inside. Turned back her way.

"What do you think happened, Miss Ziegler?"

She hadn't told him she was married. As Walker had predicted, he hadn't asked about that.

"Someone threw something through my window," she said. "A rock, I suppose. I haven't looked for it. I didn't think I should tamper with the — with the evidence, I guess you'd call it."

"It wasn't a rock. This is a bullet."

She could feign curiosity better than surprise.

"Are you sure?"

"It didn't sink deep. Must have been almost spent when it came through the glass. We'll have someone dig it out. He'll try not to do too much damage than has been done already. If they give you any trouble about your security deposit, refer 'em to the department."

He flipped his book shut. "I wouldn't worry too much about this. It's deer season. Someone fired too close to town, either with a high-powered rifle, which is illegal in this part of the state, or a muzzle-loader, which isn't; but not pointed this direction. It was probably an accident, but it's the kind we take seriously. We'll find the idiot. He won't be handling a firearm again any time soon. Odds are way on your side it won't happen again."

He pointed his notebook at the window. "I'd get in touch with the landlord and have that window boarded up right away. The weather's not going to stay this mild very long. I can feel a change coming on."

"Arthritis?" She put sympathy in her tone.

"No, ma'am. Michigan."

"They'll be back," Walker said.

The man the realty office had sent to repair the window had come and gone. She'd swept up the shattered glass and he'd spent less than five minutes nailing a square of plywood over the frame. He said a glazier would be in Monday to finish the job. Now she and Walker were sitting in the living room drinking gin. He looked piratical with a rectangle of pink plastic pasted under his left eye.

"You sound like you're talking about hostile Indians." She'd changed back into her warm quilted robe and stuck her feet in her favorite slippers. Her heart had slowed to normal, replaced with the kind of contentment that settles in after the shock of an accident has worn off and you're okay; although part of it might have been the alcohol buzz. It was like drinking hot buttered rum in the lodge after a day on the slopes.

"Indians wear warpaint. You never know when a cop's gunning for you till he drops the hammer."

She'd turned the TV on for company while he was gone. It was muted now; the Weather Channel was tracking a blizzard through the Ohio Valley that threatened to dump six to eight inches on metropolitan Detroit in the next twenty-four hours. The purple blotch kept creeping in jerky stop-motion from left to right, reversing itself, then repeating the motion. It had been a late Indian summer at that, and none of the residents the locals spoke to were as excited about the shift as the on-air talent. There was nothing like a killer storm to sweep a stand-up reporter into an anchor job.

"I checked out the park," Walker said. "The frost was gone, so I couldn't tell if anyone had walked through it or been in the gazebo. I still think he was shooting from an elevated position, most likely a roof; that bullet's too low on the wall to have been fired at an upward angle. Let the locals find *which* roof. They've got the personnel and it's what they're paid for. They'll bring in some techs from the state lab in Lansing with their calipers and measuring tape and whiz-bang three-D cameras, and when they're finished they'll know less than you and I do about who fired the shot."

"You knocked me down before it happened. Did you see something?"

"Maybe. It's hard to remember the order of things when they go that fast, but I don't think I saw movement. I'm not Spider-Man; it just seemed time for something to happen. You get a feeling for it, something building up. If I knew anything about the stock market I'd be dressing better."

"I understand the building-up part. I can't stand this waiting. How do you?"

"Patience comes with practice. Someday I hope to have it. As it is I hate this part a little more every time."

"What else can we do?"

"You? Nothing. Me?" He grinned into his glass. She'd seen more of his teeth in one day than she'd seen of Peter's since the day they'd met. She never knew when either of them was actually enjoying himself. "That stuff you told the cops," Walker said, "Heidi can't wait to get shut of the big bad city; was it just for the yokels?"

"Partly. Mostly I couldn't wait to leave the farm. You spend all your time worrying about the weather. Even when it's good, you wonder how long it'll last, and if you'll have new clothes the first day of school. When you don't, the kids who live in town swoop down on you like crows. Then there's the choice of who you'll get to spend the rest of your life with. My mother made a strong case for the boy who stood to inherit six hundred acres of soy beans. He found someone after I married Peter, a girl I grew up with. I'm expecting this year's form Christmas letter any time. Last year they were still living with his parents. One thing people in the country rarely do is die young."

"I'm guessing you're missing the bright lights."

"The lights, anyway. Most people here turn them off around eleven." She set down my glass and leaned forward. "On short acquaintance, Mr. Walker, I don't think you're any better at small talk than my husband is. This isn't a first date. Why the sudden interest in what I like and what I don't?"

"Oh, I can talk the arms off an octopus when I need to."

"Are we discussing flying the coop?"

He glanced toward the TV screen, where a young woman in a stocking cap and all-weather coat too heavy for fifty-two degrees Fahrenheit stood with her back to the Edsel Ford Freeway, shouting into a microphone over the roar of cars whipping past ten miles above the speed limit. When he turned back her way, his grin was broad, drawing a crease across the Band-Aid on his cheek.

"You're still thinking rural, Daisy Mae. I'm thinking more along the lines of a shell game, with a little help from Jack Frost."

ME

TWENTY-TWO

Dr. Chuck answered my call. My car was back where I'd left it, and the cops had gone home; my home, probably. I took another cab to Detroit and came back in my heap. After checking on Laurie I retired to my room to rest up for what Mother Nature might bring. The battery-operated radio I'd brought contained a weather band, and I tuned to it to track the storm. The NOAA announcer could barely keep awake: Cold fronts, dew points, and chill factors were a job to him, not a stepping-stone to the glamour game of network television. For once the forecasters seemed to have nailed it, as wind and snow scraped their way across the Midwestern states like a cake knife, icing lakes, laminating roads, and heaping snow up against fences, barns, and stuck cars.

It was all music to me — if we didn't end

up stuck in a snowbank with a killer on our heels.

Outside my little snuggery, the lit streets were still bare, but the wind had begun to whistle and whump up against the west wall, making the old house sway. Carpenters knew how to build them then, like poplars that gave a little before the blast and went back to vertical after it left, while stubborn oaks broke like pencils. That was before they found out that replacing roofs and siding paid more in dividends after the digging-out.

I save Dickens for nights like that. When the sun's bright and the grass is green he's just depressing; but in high weather *Bleak House* wraps you in steamer robes with a coal fire blazing in the iron hearth, and oil lamps smell as good as roasting meat. I stretched out on top of the sleeping bag with my head propped against my frayed overnighter and cracked open the cover. The snarled case of Jarndyce *v.* Jarndyce, spanning generations of litigants, attorneys, and magistrates, and page after thick, cream-colored page of handset type, kept me busy looking up words in the dictionary I'd brought. But most of them had been crowded out of the last edition by "heart-healthy," "politically correct," and "ginormous." I flung the dictionary at the wall where the storm was hitting, set aside Mr. Tulkinghorn, Lady Dedlock, William Guppy, and the rest and lit a cigarette, blowing insolent smoke at the disabled detector hanging from its wires like a giant glaring eyeball.

I thought about the fifth of Old Smuggler I'd brought, nestled on its two-by-four crosspiece; decided against it. If Roger Macklin made up his mind to launch another assault, he'd do it before heavy blowing snow got in the way of his aim, and I needed those reflexes that age and a fairly battered life had left me. I got up, popped the top off a can of tuna packed in water, and ate it with the spoon attached to my Boy Scout knife, washing it down with evaporated milk; I felt like a cat. Fish is brain food. If that wasn't advantage enough, I'd breathe in the enemy's face.

There's something about being holed up, bracing for a gale, that sharpens the senses and makes the gray cells stand on end, like tire-shredders. I put them to work on what made Laurie Macklin tick. I didn't buy into the old wheeze that today's youngsters were cosseted against the ugliness of the world and unprepared to deal with it. People come in all flavors regardless of the time and circumstances of their birth. Still, she didn't fit any sort of mold. Either she'd done a lot of growing up in the short time she'd been with her husband — anyone would, if she survived at all — or that pioneer strain you still sometimes found in children bred in the country had tempered her like the head of a good hammer. A lot of women, and just as many men, would have come apart just like her window when a bullet passed through it, but after the shock had worn off, it was as if a tree branch had broken loose and taken out the pane. A natural disaster, and not so big a one at that; nothing that couldn't be fixed in minutes with a Band-Aid and a piece of plywood.

Me, I was still spooked. But then I'd lived long enough to know everything always looks worse in the morning.

It came, when it came, with a brass band.

The wind screamed like fabric ripping, blowing snow in towering billows that turned second stories into ground floors and built patio tables into nine-tiered wedding cakes. It played jump rope with the electric lines, whipping them and twisting the wooden poles until they snapped. When it was over and the copters were cleared to fly, half the state was as dark as North Korea.

We always blame Canada for these monsters, but she's not in the same weight class as the Rockies, the Badlands, and the plains states; or for that matter little Milford, which by morning would be a tabletop village in a Christmas window display, heaped to its steeples with drifts thick as fresh-poured mortar. But by then we were long gone.

I was chasing Frosty the Snowman through an Arctic storm, waving his hat, when the first wave of snow smacked the side of the house, waking me. The luminous dial on my watch said the sun was up, but the sky lay on the ground like a fat lady with a broken ankle. She was hurling fistfuls of ice at the window to get my attention.

I flicked up the wall switch. The ceiling fixture didn't think much of that because it didn't respond. I'd packed what I'd needed before going to sleep, so I groped in the dark for my overnighter and the foul weather gear.

Laurie was up when I knocked, but just barely. She came to the door barefoot in blue flannel pajamas, no makeup, her hair matted on one side and sticking up on the other. That made her as homely as one of

Degas' ballerinas.

"It's beginning to look a lot like Christmas," I said. "Pack what you need while I warm up the buggy."

"Power's out." She sounded muzzy.

I fished the pencil flashlight out of my coat pocket and gave it to her. "Just grab what you'll need for a couple of days. We can pick up anything else. It goes on the expense account."

"I'd rather pay for it myself. Letting Peter dress me would be like —"

"Going backward. Lady, I don't care. Snap it up. When it blows like this there's no telling when it will blow past."

"Can you drive in this?"

"No one can drive in this. That's why we waited for it."

"That doesn't —"

I never found out what it didn't. I pulled her door shut and sprinted downstairs.

"What's the matter, neighbor, roof blow in?"

A man around my age, wearing the kind of pajamas you save for when everything else is in the wash, stood inside the open door of a ground-floor apartment, scratching a wild patch of gray hair with a pipe-stem. His toes looked indecent sticking out of flip-flops, as men's do.

228

I muttered something about getting my car off the street to make room for the plow. To leave him curious would be to cut Roger's reaction time when he came to find out why he hadn't seen us around.

The nose of the Cutlass stuck out of a quay of snow that was already up to my shins. The motor didn't want to start. I pumped the pedal, tried again, and it made a noise like a sick hippo. I serenaded it with lyrics from a filthy sea chantey and it fired a couple of times and caught. Then the wipers wouldn't budge, so I got out, shoving my feet into the only mud puddle in southeastern Michigan that wasn't completely frozen, and broke them free of the ice. Of course, I'd left them turned on, so I got slapped in the snoot for my trouble.

Winter Wonderland, they used to call our state: Put it on the license plates.

I went back up, and here was one woman who could put herself together in less time than it takes to watch an opera. She'd run a brush through her hair, applied paint and powder, and managed to make a bulky polar coat look like a Dior sheath. The turtleneck of what looked like the sweater she'd worn in her most recent candid photograph tickled the soft flesh under her jawbone. Quickly but with precision she scooped her hair into a red knitted beret, pulled the sides down over her ears, and picked up a small suitcase made of molded fiberglass by the handle.

She caught me staring. "What?"

"Just wondering why Macklin let you go."

She smiled then, wide as the world.

Twenty-Three

You can drive from Milford to Detroit in a little over thirty minutes. It took us two hours.

The snow was drifting across all lanes, with nothing to stop it this side of Windsor, and already the overpasses looked like something stranded in an unbroken field of white. The sun was a watery lightness in the pewter-colored overcast; you could lose it in any of the fifty-foot lamps that stood on both sides of the Chrysler freeway. They were usually shut off by that time of day. But not today.

I was in no hurry. A sixteen-ton semi was stuck in the acceleration lane like a plastic horse in a slotted track, and every quarter-mile or so an Oompa Loompa decorated the shoulder, waiting for a shovel to turn it back into an automobile. I'd timed my entry to let a big orange bronto of a county snowplow pass and we rode its polished wake all the way to Southfield, where it got off to help clear Telegraph Road. We'd clocked a steady seventeen miles per hour, but with the snow flying fast as ever — we were moving with the storm, after all — I slowed down with no one running interference.

We made no conversation during that trip. My passenger's face stuttered in and out of view as we passed the tower lights, looking like the terrified woman on an old-time paperback cover. When I saw myself in the rearview I looked like one, too.

It was as bad as things get in a state that doesn't have hurricanes or tidal waves, but it didn't stop the occasional Autobahner from cruising past us at seventy, driving a four-wheeler that performed swell in heavy snow but not on glassy pavement. We usually found him up the road, a pair of trouble lights flashing SOS from the depths of a snowdrift on the shoulder.

We slalomed a bit ourselves, once completing two thirds of a 180, luckily with no cars in our path. That was months ago, and I can still make out the impressions of Laurie's fingers in the dash on the passenger side.

As for traffic, it was less than on a usual Sunday, but nothing like the wasteland in states that don't get big snows often enough to stock the salt and equipment necessary to deal with them. Some people work weekends, and in our city you didn't let a little thing like the Blizzard of the Century keep you from punching in. If you did it once, what's to stop you from making a habit of it, and of standing in line outside the employment office?

The flakes were coming slower when we took the exit, avoiding the side streets where we could because they're the last to see a city scraper.

Laurie broke her vow of silence. "Where are we going, by the way? A hotel?"

"It isn't Miami. There aren't so many Roger can't cover them all, showing your picture to desk clerks wrapped in a C-note. I thought about my place, but these days it looks like I'm the only one who needs a key to get in. Your husband's already been there twice without being invited. He broke into my office once; but right now I think that's the one place no one will expect you to pitch a tent."

"Why would that be?"

"Because it's uncomfortable enough just sitting in it eight hours a day."

Grand River Avenue, a fairly dirty stretch of urban landscape with all the architectural innovation of an aircraft hangar, had vanished. In its place someone had smuggled in a village from the English lake country. The snow had almost stopped, the flakes turning slowly as they fell, like paper cutouts in a mobile. The sun had shouldered its way into the open, making the cloaked sidewalks sparkle. The parking meters wore elves' caps and snow hung lace curtains in the windows. The air was as clean and sharp as new steel.

It was as beautiful as we get. We paid tribute to it by saying nothing, rolling silently through the black tracks other tires had made in the white and looking through all our windows. It was temporary, which was a big part of the charm. In no time at all more tires would churn it into brown slush, stray dogs and homeless men would contribute their own personal shade of yellow, and rivers of icy dung-colored melt would pour into the gutters, gurgling and snorting like an old man with postnasal drip. But for now it was something to hang on the wall and look at on those days when you were shut in.

My building had a jump on the others. It stuck its ugly mug three stories into a sky suddenly turned achingly blue, sharpening the contrast. Horned and scaly creatures from myth spat rusty water from the roof, staining the walls a deeper shade of umber and making a moat in the snow at their base. It made the House of Usher look like the Crystal Palace.

There was no sign of my self-appointed parking valet in the deserted building across the street. I was surprised he'd hung around as long as he had; as intriguing venues go, a concrete shell filled with the ghosts of grease monkeys and dishwashers is a long way from the ruins of Troy.

The lights were on in my building. I saw it as a good sign.

We found the super plucking white plastic letters from the directory in the foyer. He looked like a Russian peasant in a political cartoon. A colony of hippies had moved out of the seat of his overalls and he was growing new cultures in the faded red handkerchief hanging like a tongue out of his hip pocket.

"Laurie Macklin, this is Rosecranz," I said. "When they built the Kremlin, he carried the hod."

"A lie. It is made of wood." I think he actually pulled his forelock when he laid eyes on my guest.

"Pleased to meet you, Mr. Rosecranz."

"Please, just Rosecranz. I came to this

country because it knows no class."

She laughed. "Classes."

"No, he got it right. Who'd we lose?" I pointed at the jumble of letters in his calloused palm with my chin.

"The tailor. In the middle of the night he left, with all his samples and two weeks' behind on the rent."

"The corporation will blame you for that."

"I am sure."

I cranked out my wallet and started counting out bills from Macklin's deck. "This should cover it. With change to spare, since you charge me more than anyone else in the building."

For answer he inclined his forehead toward the ruptures in the tile walls. Laurie looked. "Are those *bullet* holes?"

"Get yourself shot at once at work, years ago, and they never let you forget," I said. To him: "You still got that rollaway cot in your office?"

"A man must sleep."

I added a fifty to the sheaf of cash. "For this you can do it standing up, like a horse. Take it up to the tailor's, with some fresh linen. You've got a new tenant."

He looked at her again. For him she'd lost her charm.

"It is against the law."

236

"When did you start caring about zoning? You sleep here yourself and you founded a Russian province in the basement. How many relatives do you have, anyway?"

"I should send them back to Kiev?"

"I'm sure it's stopped glowing by now."

"Give it up, Amos," Laurie said. "The man doesn't want me here."

"I did not say that."

He took the bills, stuffed them in his bib pocket, and shuffled toward his door around the corner from the stairwell, walking on the outside of his feet with one knee pointing west and the other pointing east. Waiting for the cot, I shook out a cigarette and tapped it against the back of my hand.

Laurie said, "How often do you go through some version of that?"

"It isn't that bad. I don't always see him."

"Where would you have put me if the tailor hadn't moved out?"

"Look at this dump. It's off the main track in a city where anyone can afford to set up downtown. It's got more empty space than a goalie's smile, and every week they knock down another crack house and don't put up anything in its place. The tailor was on my floor; that's a break I hadn't counted on. Between that and the blizzard, our luck may be changing."

"How long am I staying?"

"As long as it takes and as short as I can make it. At the risk of bruising your feelings, the plan is to have you out long before the rent comes due. I'm not being cheap. We flung ourselves into the teeth of the storm for a reason. With you under wraps, I'm free to do some stalking of my own."

"That's not what Peter hired you for."

"So he said, at gunpoint. I'm not the waiting type, I told you that. Consider me a one-man ad hoc committee."

"First I left a house, now an apartment. What's next, a refrigerator box?"

The old fraud came back, pushing a striped mattress in a metal frame. Three of its casters squeaked and the fourth spun horizontally, like every other supermarket cart on earth. Folded double, the mattress was as thick as a mouse pad. I helped him lug it up the stairs. By the time we reached the second landing I was wheezing like a leaky calliope. He was sweating a little. To hear him tell it he'd hiked all the way from Moscow to Odessa in diapers, with Cossacks galloping close behind. That would put him in his second century, but even if it was malarkey he had the constitution of a steppe bear.

The tailor's office, down the hall and

across from mine, smelled of sizing and starch and there were enough bits of snipped thread on the floor to weave and clothe a wedding party. A beige telephone stood on the floor with the wire coiled around it. I opened the narrow door to the water closet. It had the same setup as mine, a toilet and sink and no counter, but I had a mirror above the sink. It was no bigger than the changing room in a cabana. The office itself was a good-size space, with no partition to divide a reception area from the workroom, unlike mine. The window was shaded and the light came harshly from an unfrosted bulb in a clear bowl attached to the ceiling.

"Could be worse," I said. "Ten years ago I bribed a client out of solitary in the Jackson pen. He didn't have a phone."

Rosecranz said, "It is shut off."

Laurie looked around. She'd taken off her beret and shaken loose her hair, and stood slapping her hip with the hat.

"It's not so bad. My dorm room at OSU was smaller, and I had to share it with two other girls. I could use a mirror, and access to a shower when I'm tired of taking sink baths."

"I can smuggle you into mine," I said.

The Russian shook his shaggy head. "It is no place for a lady."

"Lucky I'm not one."

I dug out another fifty. "I'd feel better if someone sat in the hall at night. There's more where this came from if it goes past three nights."

He thrust his fists in his pockets. "I am not a Bolshevik. I will sit outside her door for as long as necessary and you need not bribe me like a guard in prison."

Just when you think someone has no surprises left, he draws one like a pistol.

Which reminded me. I excused myself, let myself into my office, unlocked the safe, and returned carrying the Luger.

"I've got a gun, remember?"

"Not enough gun. A pro like Roger eats .32 slugs like peanuts."

I showed her where the safety was, racked the shell out of the barrel, slipped out the magazine and replaced it, and pumped another into the pipe. I extended it butt-first. A slender hand wrapped itself around the checked grips. She knew enough to point it at an uninhabited corner while she examined it. Rosecranz looked on, his face dark and disapproving.

"You asked about a secret knock before." I rapped the nearest wall twice, then paused, then rapped again. She aped the gesture. "If it's anything else," I said, "answer it with bullets."

■ ■ ■ ■

THEM

■ ■ ■ ■

TWENTY-FOUR

He'd slept in the 'Vette.

The storm didn't hit until the wee hours, but from the reports on the radio, confirmed by the Weather Service website on his dash computer, he couldn't be sure if he'd be able to drive back into town from the dump he was renting in Wixom. But the seat reclined, and when the cold woke him he'd started the engine and let the heater warm the interior. With a deli wrap and a bottle of Perrier — given his condition, he'd learned the importance of keeping his body tuned up as well as the car — he was content to spend the night in the parking lot of a medical building that closed at seven, getting out when necessary to relieve himself into a planter containing a young tree. He'd slept in worse places.

It amused him, when he gave thought to his rheumatic heart, to reflect upon the fact that his contempt for his mother was even stronger than his father's indifference to her. If she hadn't spent Roger's teenage years in an alcoholic haze, she'd have gotten him the treatment he needed to restore his health. When the bottle took precedence over the maternal instinct, who was the real criminal, the second-generation contract killer or the drink-sodden mother of a sick child?

But if it hadn't been for Peter Macklin, his choice of professions and the lie he lived at home — when he was home — there'd have been no bottle, and consequently no need for Roger to spend every waking moment under the shadow of death. Seeing the old man playing the hypocrite at Donna Macklin's graveside had brought his blood to a boil. How ironic would it have been had Roger's heart given out when he took a swing at the man he hated more than any other?

To top it all, the two-faced son of a bitch had had the colossal nerve to try to keep his son from the work he himself was still conducting, *then* marry a woman barely older than Roger and begin living the lie all over again.

Forcing him to pay for sparing her life, then killing her anyway and then hanging it on him; that would settle so many scores.

If — longest of long shots — the thing could be done while Macklin watched helpless would be even sweeter. But —

Killing Macklin next, in his own cell, once he'd suffered enough; now, *that* would be worth even a fatal heart attack.

He had fallen asleep and was dreaming that very thing when the blizzard hit, snatching the car between its teeth and shaking it like a dog. The Corvette rocked on its springs, a gush of snow whited out the windows and windshield, icy air found its way in through every seam in the compartment, blowing hard, grainy snow that pricked his face and neck like needles and stung his ears.

He twisted the key in the ignition, but he'd slept longer than he'd thought; the fan blew nothing but cold at his feet. He switched it off while the motor warmed up, then opened all the vents, turned his collar up around his ears, and slid down onto his spine with his knees pressed against the dash and his arms folded with his hands in his armpits. The driving gloves he wore were uninsulated and helpless against frostbite. He turned on the radio for the distraction.

"This storm is moving rapidly. . . ."

"No shit, Stephen Hawking." He scanned through more End-of-Days voices, squirming nests of rap, and a horde of talk shows, stopping at last on an R-and-B station. But every fresh gust brought static. He bailed out and listened to the wind climb and fall and ice crystals rattling against the finish.

The snow swept past in clouds, smacking the side of the car in waves and rocking it on its springs. The motion and the monotony put him to sleep.

When he woke, the storm had blown out of town. Winter advisories remained in force to the east, with countless reports of vehicles wrecked or stranded. Meanwhile, in the village, peace reigned. Snow swaddled it in eerie silence. Even the constant thrum of freeway traffic had ceased, apart from the rumble of heavy trucks pushing snow and spraying brine.

He had to heave his weight against the door to break loose the ice, and when he got out with his brush and scraper he saw the fall had turned its clean lines into something resembling a plush toy. He dug out the exhaust pipe first to prevent an ice ball from sealing it, and as the blue-gray smoke appeared and the heat melted a dirty hole in the white drift, he used the brush to push the heavy snow off the roof, hood, and trunk, then the scraper to clear the windshield and windows of ice softened by the blower inside.

All this helped him stay on point. If his resentment hadn't gotten to the point where it interfered with his sleep, he'd still be in Miami Beach, where he owned a condo, or vacationing in Vegas, where a hotel manager who was paying down his debt to one of Roger's associates kept a suite vacant (and off the registry) for important visitors. Just because a man was born and reared in Michigan — Siberia West — didn't mean he had to put up with mukluks and mittens five months out of the year. The amount he spent running the Corvette through a car wash twice a week to keep the slush and road salt from eating holes in the undercarriage was better dumped on the craps table, which at least was entertaining.

When he was finished he put the car in gear, gunned it to shove his way through the accumulation, and turned into the street, which was relatively clear; some civic-minded citizen was already at work on the cross street in a pickup with rusty wheel wells and a blade up front.

Roger circled Laurie Macklin's apartment house. The window facing the park was covered with plywood. He'd hoped to frighten off her watchdog yesterday, aiming his rifle, a lightweight bolt-action target piece made in South Africa, high; to kill Walker, or even wing him, would make his primary mission ten times more difficult. In Detroit or Miami, a day without a homicide, or an attempt at one, was as rare as a bishop's fart, but in little candy-ass Milford it would bring on a full-court police press. There were a lot fewer doors to knock on there, and cars passing through to stop and search. A wild shot with no casualties was another species entirely. The rural Midwest had two seasons, hunting and target practice, and any shithead who could afford to own a rifle could point it and shoot. The local media would cover the mishap, the law would run it out, maybe even find the roof of the aerobics studio from which the bullet had been fired; but with no tracks to follow and no fingerprints left behind and the rifle itself in pieces at the bottom of Sherwood Lake east of the village — and now a fresh layer of ice to discourage dragging even if the budget stretched that far — the incident would soon fade from the collective memory.

He ranged as far as five blocks around the old house. There was no sign of Walker's car. That was encouraging. Even if Roger was leery about extending his recon into the streets that hadn't been plowed yet, he was relatively certain the man's age and game leg would keep him from parking any farther away. Either he'd been scared off or had set up shop at a distance to avoid drawing any more fire Laurie's way.

At length Roger pulled into the curb on the other side of the park and cut the motor. With nothing but an open gazebo standing between him and the house, he could see everyone who entered or left it.

He'd brought his handgun, a High Standard autoloader with a five-and-a-half-inch barrel, in a steel lockbox with a magnetic lid that sealed it to the metal superstructure under the passenger's seat, where only a thorough search would turn it up, but he wasn't going to use it yet; not at least until he'd prodded his father with another photograph of his child bride and heard back (or not) from him. He'd broken with Peter's example of ditching his weapon after use, and with his prejudice in favor of revolvers. The High Standard, a custom piece built to his order, came with interchangeable barrels, which defied ballistics tests based on striations, and spare firing pins, which made comparing spent shells useless. Although the original caliber was .22, a load that contributed to accuracy because of the light recoil, he'd had the frame reinforced to accommodate .38 and .44. After he'd employed one, he got rid of the barrel and kept the pistol. That eliminated the need to test a new weapon every time. Acquiring a replacement barrel, expensive as that was, was less costly than replacing the gun. Also it exposed him to less hazard. Peter seldom used the same armorer twice in a row, and the wider you ranged in that part of the underworld, the greater the chance of betrayal. Roger's guy was too highly placed in the munitions industry to risk his position by blowing the whistle. The profit he made from repeat business outweighed blackmail and the risk involved. It gave the son satisfaction to know he'd improved on his father's methods.

The clouds slid eastward all of a piece, like someone shoving open a door on tracks. The sun was summer-bright, glaring off the impeccably white earth and forcing him to hook on his designer shades. Traffic picked up, the first of a succession of snow-blowers announced itself with a tug and a whirr and another tug and then the kettle-drum tympani of pistons chugging into action. The village plows started on the lesser-used side streets; more privately owned trucks, some with magnetic advertising signs on the sides of the cabs, started in on the parking lots. A white-bearded jasper wearing four kinds of plaid and knee-high boots came out of a house, pulling a box sled containing a power augur and a bouquet of short fishing rods down the sidewalk, headed for some frozen fishing hole; the damn fool thought the ice would be thick enough to support him on the strength of a three-hour cold spell. Roger was reminded it was Sunday, and to linger too long might attract attention from stay-at-home neighbors. But he expected Laurie to come out any time. It was that kind of day, brisk and bright and built for strolling through the dear old village, breathing in the clean air and admiring the holiday decorations. He reached into the backseat to scoop up his camera bag, screwed the long lens onto the Nikon, and with the sun warming the interior of the car sat back to soak it in while he waited.

Macklin said, "What good's an intelligence professional who can't provide intelligence?"

"I wish you'd keep your voice down."

"I keep it down for a living. Answer the question."

They were sitting in the corner of a dive in Mt. Clemens, a hike north of Detroit, where the chances of their being recognized were small. The bar itself had been shuttered twice for serving alcohol to minors and once for solicitation of prostitution, and reopened by way of an arrangement with an assistant city manager who'd been forced to resign soon after for his understanding nature. It was dark by design, the walls painted forest green and the only illumination courtesy of candle lamps on the tables and the wash from the working light above the bar. The establishment was the local venue of choice for stray spouses and closeted gentry. A CD juke played a succession of 1980s rock, low enough so that the pulse of the basses barely penetrated the murmur of low conversation. The air was a fug of beer and deep-fried carcinogens.

The man seated across from Macklin was built like an NFL lineman gone to seed. His face, shoulders, and waist were broad, but in such proportion that few people realized just what a tub of lard he was until he stood or sat next to someone of average height and weight. His neck and his head were as much of one piece as a fireplug. To minimize the risk of recognition in that company, he'd left behind his suit and tie — still the FBI uniform forty years after the death of J. Edgar Hoover — and wriggled into XXXL jeans, a muckety-dung sweatshirt, and a lumberman's jacket with a red-

and-black check; a mistake, that coat: It made him look more enormous yet. No wonder he rode a desk. He'd stick out in the field like a parade float.

"I'm underutilized," he said. "I'm a federal official with clearance all the way up to the attorney general. I don't know why I had to drive the hell and gone this far to do something for you that you could get from the Secretary of State's office in Lansing."

"That was the first call I made. There's no record Roger registered a vehicle in Michigan, and I shouldn't have to tell *you* it's a lot harder to do it under a phony name and Social Security number than it was before nine-eleven. I don't have contacts in all fifty states. If I did I'd never get through them all in time."

"It's a states' rights issue. If I pull rank it'll cause a stink."

"I shouldn't have to remind you I can stink up the place all on my own."

"Not without exposing yourself."

Macklin laughed rarely, and never when he was truly amused. He did so now. "How you got so high knowing so little is a mystery."

The agent turned the beer glass in front of him between his palms. It looked like a thimble by comparison. "Where should I start?"

Macklin paid for the drinks, slipped an extra sheaf of bills under a paper coaster, and stood, unhooking the windbreaker from the back of his chair. "Florida and Nevada. He's a snowbird. Get me the make, model, and plate number and I'll do the rest." He looked down at the other man. God, he was fat. "You're sweating for nothing. It isn't Watergate."

"You're right. No one was killed in Watergate."

■ ■ ■ ■

ME

■ ■ ■ ■

Twenty-Five

I left Laurie to feather the nest I'd scooped out for her and went back to my office to make a call, converting the mail under the slot to trash on the way. Barry Stackpole answered on one ring. Caller ID has its blessings as well as its faults.

"Why are you still haunting that flea palace?" he greeted. "Don't you know the whole world works at home? They're storing hay in the Empire State Building."

"I ask myself that question first of every month. Then once or twice a year something comes along to answer it. Just now I'm using it to violate a city ordinance."

"You can't fight the Coleman A. Young Municipal Center."

"I can spar with it. I need a picture."

"Take a selfie."

"As close to current a shot as you can get of one Roger Macklin."

"Sounds like a baseball player. What's he

done, and when can I shout it to the world?"

Barry was the last living investigative reporter. Thirty years had passed since he almost lost that title. As it was he came out of it with three limbs, eight fingers, and nine-tenths of his skull. These days he was doing his shouting over the World Wide Web.

"You're slipping, cuz. He may be the latest addition to a fine old family firm, but he's been there long enough to make a few sales."

"Macklin, right. We haven't heard from Peter in a while. Last I heard he was rooting for the Blue Jays."

Toronto. "You dog. How long have you and Deb Stonesmith been dating?"

"She's married to the chief; the way Sister Mary Immaculata's married to Jesus. But now and then we run into each other in the line at Krispy Kreme. Seems to me your name came up in that conversation. You don't call, you don't write. I'm going to buy you a computer just so I can unfriend you."

I let that dangle. "I know the feds have a photo on file at least as recently as when they buried Peter's ex, because Roger threw a fist at him in the cemetery, but I don't know how long ago that was."

"Sec." A sound came over the line like dice rattling in a cup, and I knew he was logged in. "Year ago last month. I'll see if I can dig up something fresher. Am I wasting time asking why?"

"Only if my obituary shows up before I get back to you."

He started to say something else, but I got the razz from the waiting room. Someone had opened the hall door, activating the buzzer. A shadow shapelier than the usual came to the pebbled glass. I made sure Barry had all my current contact numbers, hung up, and told her to come on in.

"I hope I'm interrupting." She'd changed from the sweater and slacks into something in rayon or heavy silk, a one-piece dress that showed off her trim athletic figure. "I feel like I'm freeloading on all your hard work and you need a break."

"I took mine in October and November. Demand's down since Bill Gates started giving away information for free." I rose partway and jerked an elbow toward the chair on the customer's side. She swept into it and crossed her legs. She wore sheer stockings or possibly Coppertone and low-heeled pumps. I couldn't identify the scent she wore. Juniper, maybe. Or maybe I was just remembering her good gin.

"I like your office. It doesn't stand for any nonsense. No Zen garden, no clickety-click metal balls. My old boss at the travel agency had a putting green *and* a basketball hoop."

"I'd get more mileage out of a firing range, but I don't have the room. Settled in?"

"As much as I can be. I think that roll-away is stuffed with Russian thistle."

"The CPA on the second floor has a leather recliner. I'll see if I can borrow it."

"Please don't. I'm enough bother as it is."

This was where I should say she was no bother at all. I played with a cigarette and said nothing.

If she was disappointed, she didn't show it. She stroked one of the chair's walnut arms. "I suppose you think I'm naïve or stupid or both."

"Does it matter what I think?"

Her smile this time was bitter. "That answers my question. Would it help you make up your mind which if I tell you I still love Peter?"

"Nope."

"Why not?"

"I read poetry."

"Is that supposed to mean something?"

"Love and smarts have nothing to do with each other. I think it was Wordsworth said it. Or maybe it was a fortune cookie. I mix them up all the time."

"Well, I won't bore you with a list of Peter's good traits."

"Thanks."

She looked as if I'd slapped her. Then she decided to get mad. She pushed herself to her feet and smoothed her skirt.

"Don't forget to slam the door on your way out," I said.

She had her hand on the knob. She turned back, thought about getting madder, then suddenly let out a gust of laughter. She went out, closing the door gently behind her.

That made three times in one day. Either she was getting positively giddy or I had a stand-up act to fall back on when sleuthing played out.

I waited for the phone to ring. I didn't know if Barry would find what I needed in five minutes or five days. I tore the spent days off the daily calendar on the desk and sent it off after last week's mail. I lit the cigarette. The smoke clawed at my stomach lining and I remembered something. I locked up, went to the tailor's old office, code-knocked, and waited while she unlocked. I had a key just in case, but I didn't want to be shot by my own Luger. She'd taken off her shoes. Like most women she'd found a way to turn an industrial space into a country cottage. Her rigid suitcase stood

263

on end next to the rollaway, supporting a gooseneck lamp I recognized from Rosecranz's office. A gauzy pink scarf embroidered with yellow buds was draped over the copper shade, diffusing the harsh light.

There were other improvements. A thick woolen blanket covered the rollaway with a giant pillow on top of it. Either one took up too much space to have come in her bag.

"If you came to forgive me, I accept," she said.

I didn't have anything half so clever, so I watched it walk the waters.

"The fairy godmother's been in, I see. That spread doesn't go with anything in that supply closet the old Cossack hangs out in."

"He went out and bought them for me. Wasn't that sweet?"

"Like borscht. On that subject, it just hit me I haven't had anything to eat since some Chicken of the Sea sushi last night. Want to catch a bite?"

"That drive through the Yukon wore me out. Why don't you wake me up and surprise me with something?"

"You've got only yourself to blame if it turns out to be liver and onions."

"Love 'em."

I pulled my head out of the room and waited until I heard the lock snap. Considering how she loved in general, liver and onions came as no surprise.

The Hockeytown Cafe on Woodward laid out a takeaway spread of burgers, barbecue, and deli sandwiches that could stop your heart just by reading the menu. I bought a meatball sub, a lean Reuben, a pulled-pork sandwich, a quart of coleslaw and a quart of potato salad, and stopped at a market on John R for a six-pack of Purple Gang, a local brew, from the coldcase. It wouldn't go to waste even if she didn't like beer.

When she didn't answer her door after the second knock, I took a chance and used the key. I opened the door just far enough to see she was lying on her side under the woolen blanket, stirring it with the even action of her lungs. She was smiling in her sleep. She'd said to wake her, but unlike the case with a nightmare you can never pick up a good dream where you left off. I eased the door shut and carried the greasy bag and carton down the hall into my waiting room, where someone was waiting who I really didn't want to see.

TWENTY-SIX

He was sitting on the padded bench, reading a magazine from the assortment I set out to make the place look uptown, folded back to the middle. From what I saw of his face under the brim of his winterweight Trilby, his lips didn't move.

"Working Sundays," he said. "Lord's day off; tsk-tsk."

"You, too, Detective. No rest for the worried."

He snapped the magazine shut and swatted it with his free hand. "We're going to war in Iraq, it says here. Old Uncle Saddam's in for a spanking."

"Funny, Detective. It may not be this month's *Vogue,* but I don't keep them around any longer than a term in the Senate." I wrestled the six-pack under the arm supporting the sack of food and shook out my keys.

Stan Kopernick looked up. The heavy

handsome jaw was working, but I didn't think he had any gum. "Expecting company?"

"Me and my reflection in a beer bottle. I'm past due addressing my Christmas cards. If I don't get 'em in the mail before closing, they'll be late."

"You don't have that many friends. All the time I'm sitting here I heard your phone ring once."

A muscle jumped in my cheek. If Barry had called back and left a message, he might have heard it. On the other hand, Barry never put anything on the record that might be overheard and put to use.

"Marketing. You know, 'Wishing you a season without a case to crack. A. Walker Investigations.' "

"Sounds counterproductive."

"It's a subliminal message. Come on in. Meatballs or corned beef? I'm saving the pulled pork for myself."

He rose to his full height, patting his thick hard stomach. The camel's-hair coat hung open over what looked like the same blue suit. "Jenny Craig's got me on a low-carb diet: Fitness review next month. But I'll take some suds."

Inside the office, he raised his head an inch, and with it the bold nose; sniffed. "I thought you was a Scotch man. Gin's a cheap drunk."

"There's no such thing." I wasn't fooled for a minute. He bought that the juniper scent came from a liquor store the way I bought the Ambassador Bridge.

"You got a message." He pointed at the light blinking on the answering machine.

I looked at the ID: BLOCKED CALL. Barry left fewer tracks than a seaplane.

"Cremation service," I said, setting the sack of sandwiches between him and the screen. "You'll be getting them soon enough."

"Waste of energy. My old man worked ten years with the fire department. Burned to death in an arson fire during the riots. One pile of ashes in the family plot is more than enough."

We sat. I got the brass knuckles I used for an opener out of a drawer, pried the tops off two bottles, and slid one his way.

"Here's to crime. I'd be out of a job otherwise." Holding the bottle by the neck between thumb and finger, he tilted it and dumped half the contents down his throat. He had a delicate belch for a big man. Wiping his lips with the back of his hand he said, "I didn't think you could top that deal on I-seventy-five. I nearly tanked your pet

PhD for obstruction when we pulled him over in your car. A bust like that could get me some ink in the student paper at Wayne State. They'd be calling me Professor down at Thirteen Hundred."

Dr. Chuck hadn't told me about that, but I'd been in a hurry to get back to Milford. "He's an amateur Indiana Jones, unlocking the mysteries of old Detroit. I wasn't using it, so I thought it might help him get around to more explorations."

"A pain in the ass is what he is, him and his whole tribe. Most of them places are posted. Between the scrap rats and the urban explorers, B-and-E's getting to look like the penny arcade. What were you using for wheels while he was out joyriding in that bucket of rust? Nobody's seen you here or at your crib in days."

"You mean you and your partner haven't. We've established I can scrape you off my heel any time I take the whim."

The point was to get him sore enough to forget all about smelling Laurie Macklin's perfume; but cops don't get mad the way you and I do. They've been called coppers and flat-feet and pigs and worse, and all it does is make them yawn. If you really want to know what gets their whiskers, take a swing at one. It'll make you a dash-cam celebrity overnight.

He stirred finally, reaching for the sack on the desk. "What the hell, I got four weeks. Corned beef, you said?"

"Reuben, actually."

"Better do meatball. I like Kraut but it don't like my gut." He stuck a paw inside the sack and lifted out one of the wrapped sandwiches. "You're not hungry?"

I shook my head and drank beer. "It's a little early for me. I've got a string of calls to make and might not get the chance to go out later."

"Christmas cards, you said."

"That too. Also I haven't changed the oil in my electric razor since Labor Day."

"Take my advice. Don't eat Hockeytown meatballs cold. They squash the leftovers and use 'em for pucks." He buried his face in the sandwich, catching the dripping sauce in the wrapper. The small white cicatrix on his chin twitched as he chewed. It fascinated me. "The lady lieutenant's getting impatient. Seems the brass in Ottawa is cranking up the heat on the U.S. State Department about an American lifetaker breaching the borders. The State Department's cranking up the heat on the U.S. Attorney General, the AG's cranking up the heat on the FBI, and as you know the DPD's been wearing the feds like a coat since all them rape kits went past their sell-by date a few years back."

"I thought they'd closed that investigation."

"Just pulled the door to. Macklin's an old Combination man, made in Detroit like cars used to be, and that Lennert deal up north had him all over it. Just between you, me, and this here sandwich, Stonesmith dropped the ball when she pulled the surveillance from his soon-to-be ex; thought the divorce took her off the A-list. When she dusted soon after, that was a red flag. Could be coincidence, but I've swung court-ordered search warrants on less than that. If she's gone back to him, there's a harboring rap we might use to get her to spill what she knows, and if she didn't, we still want to talk to her, because she cleared out of Southfield in a hurry and that's probable cause to can her as a material witness. These clam babies tend to open up when they get a whiff of the air down at County."

I turned my bottle around in the permanent ring on the desk. "Hear, hear, Detective. If you're practicing this speech on me and my opinion counts."

"I ain't one of your urban explorer pals. I don't come to this dump to admire the

271

crown moldings. You pulled a boner when you tapped the lieutenant for dope on Macklin. That put you into the orbit of an international homicide investigation. Personally I don't give a rat's ass if we extradite him to them hosers in Ontario. They don't reciprocate when a death-penalty state asks for the same thing, on account of they think everybody should have a crack at old age, even a baby-killer. What I think doesn't blow up anybody's skirt downtown. Stonesmith says fetch, I fetch."

He took two more bites, obliterating two-thirds of the sandwich, mopped his lips with a brown paper napkin, crumpled the sandwich inside the paper, and stood, dumping it and the napkin back into the sack. He glanced at the electric wall clock that had come with the office. "It's ten A.M. You got till ten A.M. tomorrow to produce Laurie Macklin or provide us with a current address. If you do that and she hasn't pulled another dust job, you won't have to take her place in the eight-by-ten. They don't serve deli in the cafeteria. What the chefs do to that roadkill venison the sheriffs give out makes Spam seem like prime rib."

I grinned at him. "Do you rehearse this stuff or make it up on the fly? I ask because the Rotary Club invites me to its annual dinner every year and I'm running out of excuses not to share all my trade secrets over the sherbet. I can refer them to you."

Still nothing. He was as easy to rile as a loaf of bread. "Don't waste your time trying to duck the leash again. As of this morning we're double-teaming you on all three shifts. Two cars apiece, no waiting. You're an expensive guy to have around."

I followed him out at a safe distance. Watching through the crack in the hall door I thought he paused outside the former tailor's shop before taking the stairs. I couldn't tell if he'd sniffed the air and I didn't know if it was enough to swing a court-ordered search warrant.

The phone was ringing when I pulled my head back in.

"Why the delay?" Barry asked, as soon as I picked up. "I thought you wanted this pronto."

"I've got all the time in the world now. I just found out I'm the grand marshal in a police parade."

"Stonesmith?"

"Her pet Neanderthal."

"Kopernick? I heard he'd transferred. Don't underestimate the species. They had bigger brains than us. So is it a wash?"

"You got the picture?"

"A good one. He took out a passport, and these days it has to be in your name. I guess he's outsourcing mayhem abroad."

I told him as much about the case as I could afford. Barry's goodwill goes only so far before you have to cough up something he can play with. "He's been hanging around Milford. I wanted to circulate the picture there, get a line on his migratory pattern, but I can't do that now without an official escort."

"Just you? The town isn't that small. It would take a week."

"I just thought of something. You going to be around for a while?"

"I'm always around, pal." He clicked off.

I pushed down the plunger and made a call. The dial tone purred four times. I was getting jumpy when Dr. Chuck came on.

"Sorry about that," he said. "I was up to my elbows in some interesting trash in Hudson's basement. That's all that's left of the place."

"How many of you are there?"

"That I know personally? Eight or ten, counting me. What's up?"

I told him.

"Milford? Where's that?"

I told him that, too.

"I don't know. Not much pickings in those

274

little burgs."

"My client's got deep pockets. I can finance a month's expedition here in town."

He liked that fine. I told him to stand by and called Barry back. "Can you run off ten prints of that photo?"

"As many as you need. I don't have to go to Photo Shack."

I gave him the rest and got the urban explorer back on the line. He repeated Barry's address and said he'd round up his crew. When we were finished I dragged over the sack and unwrapped the meatball sandwich while it was still warm. I was suddenly hungry.

■ ■ ■ ■

THEM

■ ■ ■ ■

Twenty-Seven

Change of plans.

There would be no payoff to worsen the sting. New dynamic. Laurie's murder would have to take place without Macklin bearing witness.

Three different parties came out of the house while Roger was watching, spaced ten to twenty minutes apart. One was the wrong age, two the wrong sex. The last, a coot with dirty gray hair coiling out from under his stocking cap, galoshes unbuckled and jingling, slopped around behind the building, came out with a snow shovel, and started in on one of the piles in the little lot marked RESIDENTS ONLY. Roger decided to check inside.

There was a buzzer in the shallow foyer. None of the slips next to the buttons said Laurie Macklin; but he'd already connected her to L. Ziegler in 310.

He tried a couple of buttons, but no one

buzzed back. The lock was a slip latch; a common design flaw in automatic locks. He sneezed it open with a piece of plastic he carried in his wallet.

The same dodge got him inside 310. There were clothes hanging in the closet, with empty spaces on the rod; that was inconclusive. On the floor stood two suitcases, a large and a medium, with a gap between them, where a third bag might have stood that was smaller yet, an overnighter.

Next he'd checked the bathroom. More spaces among the bottles on the counter, no toothbrush or toothpaste in the medicine cabinet.

Five minutes after letting himself in he'd come galloping downstairs and didn't slow down until he was behind the wheel. There would be no fresh picture to tack to his final ransom demand. Satisfaction would have to come with shedding blood only.

"Walker." It came out between his teeth as he stuck his key in the ignition.

But he started up gently and didn't spin rubber peeling away from the curb. With the place so quiet under its fall of snow, any show of haste on the street would draw too much fire. At the entrance to I-96 he waited, fingers drumming the wheel, while a double-bottom semi made its wide sloppy swing onto the ramp coming from the other direction, then fell in behind, passing it across the V where the acceleration lane merged with the freeway. By then there'd been enough traffic to warm the asphalt, melting the snow and ice, and he drove east toward Detroit at the customary ten miles above the limit. But on Sunday he had enough room between himself and the cars up ahead to free the magnetic box that held his High Standard from under the passenger seat and switch to the .44 barrel one-handed.

Macklin was watching the weather reports on TV when the phone rang in his condo in Warren. No greetings were exchanged, but he recognized the voice of his fat FBI contact.

"Dade County, Florida. He registered it under his own name. Two thousand thirteen Corvette, blue in color."

What else would it be blue in? Macklin thought, writing down the registration number. He hung up without having said a word.

He'd left the TrailBlazer in the private carport he'd paid for, but enough snow had drifted in to cover the windshield. He started it up and switched on the defroster, using the washer-wipers to clear away the rest.

He'd memorized the address he'd been given a few days earlier. It belonged to a Quonset-like truss building in Belleville, close enough to Detroit Metropolitan Airport for jetliners to crisscross the sky above it with white trails, turning it into a tic-tac-toe board. A nearly constant roar of air traffic shook its metal walls as planes took off in a convict line; the blizzard had grounded them and they were playing catch-up. It was painted snot-green, with a wooden sign running the width of the frontage facing the road, reading ACE'S BODY SHOP. Another sign, in faded red Sharpie on tacked-up white foam-board, said HONK TO ENTER. He braked in front of a garage door with frosted glass panes and did as directed.

After a moment something clunked, ice broke with a pop, and the door rose slowly as smoke, on chains and rollers that clanked and clattered loud enough to drown out the air traffic directly overhead. Inside, a square scow of a Cadillac Eldorado thirty years old with a dull gold finish perched on a lift and a showroom-quality Dodge Viper with easily eight coats of hand-polished paint — the kind that changed color according to the light — was parked on rubber pads on the concrete floor on the other side. There was just room enough to ease the TrailBlazer between them and get out.

The place smelled of grease, steel tools, and kerosene from a heating stove the size of a refrigerator venting smoke outside through a pipe. The air was warm. A dark dumpy man, young-old, in stained Carhartt coveralls and a flat-topped once-white cotton beanie like house-painters wore, lowered the door at the touch of a button. Coveralls and the man inside them were indescribably filthy. He wiped his hands on an equally filthy rag, with no apparent effect on his black-stained fingers, and switched off a boombox radio wrapped in protective silver duct tape in the middle of a hoarse screaming aria from the ghetto. He'd had it cranked up loud enough to be heard above the soaring jets, and after that the noise of the turbines was almost pleasant.

"Ace?" Macklin asked.

"There ain't one. But 'Schuyler's Body Shop' don't track. You Peters?"

"Yeah."

"Who sent you, Billings?"

"There ain't one." No irony rang in his tone. "Dorfman."

" 'Kay. I got to be careful. One more drop

and they carry me out of the pen feet foremost."

Macklin inclined his head toward the Viper. "Chop shop?"

"Strictly up-and-up. What'd I say? Two rackets makes twice as many ways to take a fall."

"I was thinking the same thing."

Schuyler stuffed the rag in a hip pocket and rolled a red-enamel tool cart away from the wall next to a workbench littered with tailpipes and things. He grunted with the effort; the drawers were plainly loaded down with hardware. "ATF spooks all got bad backs," he explained.

This exposed a metal heat register that didn't belong in a building with a freestanding stove. The man knelt, took hold of it with both hands, and lifted it free. From the space between walls he drew a rusty green toolbox and banged it to the floor.

His customer studied the revolvers, semiautomatic pistols, and suppressers in the box, then selected a Ruger New Model .357 Magnum, the Blackhawk, and a box of shells. Schuyler directed him to test-fire it into a seat cushion from a 1950 Oldsmobile, torn and leaking horsehair. Macklin timed it to coincide with a jet taking off directly above the roof. He pronounced the trigger pull satisfactory and the sight straight. This time there was no dickering; he hadn't time. He paid for the weapon and left, bound north to I-96 and then west toward Milford.

The private cop lived in a one-story dump on the Detroit side of Hamtramck, square except for an attached garage that had probably been added since it was built sometime during the Industrial Revolution. With fresh snow heaped all around and on the roof, all it lacked was gingerbread. A small Christmas tree stood unlit on a table in a front window.

Roger parked around the corner, lopsided on a granulated pile pushed up by a city plow, and made his way back on foot, the High Standard tucked in the reinforced pocket he'd had built into his peacoat. No light showed through any of the windows, but it was a sunny day. He peered through a garage window, cupping his hands around his eyes. No car was parked inside.

He went around to the narrow backyard, which faced the blind wall of a house fronting on the next street over. This place was nearly identical to Walker's, but no garage. There was no car in the driveway it shared with its neighbor next door. The drive had been shoveled. Most likely everyone was at church; it was that kind of neighborhood.

The snow soaked his trousers as far as his calves, but he waded through it, mounted a step, peered through the small square single-paned window in a door to what looked like a shallow back porch that had been walled in and roofed to shelter an automatic washer and dryer, another afterthought. The door rattled loosely when he tugged on the knob. It would be fastened with a hook, but a strip of half-round dowel prevented him from sliding his piece of plastic through the seam and lifting it out of the eye. He looked around, drew his pistol, pushed in the pane with an elbow, crooked his free arm inside, found the hook, and freed it.

The unheated back room was musty-smelling, with an underlay of detergent and bleach. A dead bolt secured the door to the house. He was less handy with a set of picks than with his plastic strip, but after five minutes and curses beneath his breath the two times he dropped one of the tools the bolt slid into its socket with a chunk.

There'd been noise, so he exploded through the door, wheeling right and left gripping the High Standard in both hands. A little linoleum-paved kitchen and breakfast nook yawned back, empty.

The same with a living room, decorated once by someone but that had the air of a place where no one had actually looked at the wall art and knickknacks in years. Freestanding bookshelves, a couple of dirty ashtrays, a TV and cable box, the midget tree hung with cheap ornaments, an over-stuffed chair and sofa, side table ringed all over on top like the Olympic flag, and in the air a tired blend of stale cigarettes and old cooking odors from the kitchen.

In the little bedroom an unmade bed, more books, and a plain dresser. He opened a closet with two suits hanging inside and a pair of brown shoes. His man would be wearing the black. Roger left the drawers alone. Walker and Laurie wouldn't be hiding in the drawers.

He let himself out the way he'd come, holding the pistol down behind his hip in case anyone was looking. No one was.

He had one more place to check.

Cranking the 'Vette around the corner onto Joseph Campau, Hamtramck's main stem, he hit a patch of ice and slued across the dividing line, barely missing the fender of a maroon TrailBlazer coming his way in the lane opposite, causing the driver to brake and cheat the other direction; but Roger turned into the skid without braking, corrected his course, and drove on, not looking back.

It swung around the corner in a blue streak. Macklin saw the shine on the pavement, like metal where the sun hit it, and reacted simultaneously with the driver of the sports car, touching the brake pedal lightly just to slow his momentum and flirting the wheel right even as the other let his own tires slide to *his* right. They missed each other by inches.

There was no time to read the plate, but he knew the car was the blue Corvette Roger had bought in Florida; in that neighborhood, where Amos Walker lived, no other explanation applied. He was too late. Again.

He'd wasted little time in Milford. One of the suitcases Laurie had packed when she'd left him was gone from the apartment, and so her with it. The next logical place was Walker's house. Somehow, possibly with the help of the snowstorm, he'd spirited her away from under Roger's nose.

But Roger had come to the same conclusion.

When Macklin parked in front of the house, he expected to find nothing inside but a corpse, and likely two.

Footsteps in the snow led around to the

back. This time there would be no need to hoist himself through the garage window. The window in the door to the enclosed porch was broken, the hook undone and the bolt securing the connecting door to the house disengaged. Just in case Walker was still breathing and armed, he went in holding the Ruger. The detective would be expecting Roger to come back and finish the job. He might, at that.

He'd seen everything before, studied it in order to form a more thorough picture of Walker's character, so there was no need to linger in any room. The house was deserted, with no signs of a struggle. He reversed his steps, leaving everything as it was, and when he was sure no one was waiting for him outside he stuck the revolver in his belt under the windbreaker.

He knew where Roger was headed. He kicked the TrailBlazer to life and made a U-turn back toward the freeway. His tires spun briefly on snow that had melted and refrozen. He drove one-handed, dialing Walker's office line with the other on his cell. It was busy.

■ ■ ■ ■

HER

■ ■ ■ ■

TWENTY-EIGHT

She awoke from deep in a dream that took a minute to shake. In it, her father was still alive and although she knew he'd died, she'd assumed the news hadn't reached him yet and she was agonizing over whether to tell him or just enjoy his company while it lasted. When she sat up, looked around, and remembered where she was, she was equal parts relieved and in mourning all over again. She'd been too much of late in the care of men.

It was a funny old building, square as a barn with architectural features that must have seemed quaint even at the time of construction. The walls were wavy where the lath was wearing through the plaster, or where the plaster had shrunk to the lath, so that she seemed to be living inside a square rib cage. The sun was melting the snow on the flat roof and she heard water gushing out of the downspouts shaped like gargoyles.

The tailor's shop Walker had set her up in retained much of the character of that profession. Smooth lacquered shelves covered much of one wall to a height of four feet, stripped of the bolts of silk and flannel and wool worsted that went into the making of suits. On another wall, a paper chart displayed a spread-eagled figure that reminded her of da Vinci's naked anatomical man, but dressed in a patchwork pattern of gray, white, and black swatches of fill material, which in turn made her think of a stylized hog in a butcher's shop with the loins, chops, rump, shoulder, and belly marked off by dotted lines and labeled in red ink. Motes of cotton lint swam in the blade of sunlight leaking around one edge of the windowshade, getting into her nostrils and making her sneeze.

So which was she, the kept creature awaiting slaughter or the irritant in her keeper's nose?

She swung her feet to the floor, which was cold and made her shiver, groped with them for her slippers, and got up to unhook her warm quilted robe from the back of a wooden chair. Every lump in the fusty old mattress had left a sore spot where it had pressed against her muscles. She put on the robe, swinging it above her head and shov-

ing both arms into the sleeves simultaneously. Peter had always been fascinated by
that. He put on his shirt and coat one sleeve
at a time. He couldn't figure out how she
did it the way she did, and she couldn't
explain it.

That was the kind of thing you remembered most often. Not the killing or the running away from killers or personal knowledge of people who killed (or even for that
matter of *having* killed). She couldn't get
away from those things even through sepa-
ration and divorce, and yet what kept coming back to her was the way she put on her
robe and her estranged husband's reaction
to it. Life was absurd, and death was ludi-
crous.

The pistol Walker had given her lay atop
the upended suitcase beside the copper desk
lamp. Ugly. Not like an ungainly hunk of
metal, but sleek and deadly; ugly that way,
like too many of the men Peter associated
with, the detective included. It sucked all
the cheer out of the room.

In the little water closet she used the
toilet, a white porcelain water-guzzler that
roared like a jet plane when she flushed it
and practically sucked paint off the ceiling.
Rosecranz had brought her a small square
mirror made of polished tin, a man's shav-

ing accessory, with a wire bail that hung on a nail above the sink. She laughed when she saw her reflection: sheet-creases on one side of her face, her hair standing at attention on one side and sprawled flat on the other. A fright wig in a Halloween store: The Bed-Head From Hell.

The sink had no counter, but she'd laid out her necessaries on the toilet tank. A few splashes of water and some cleansing cream smoothed out the wrinkles, but they were disturbingly similar to her mother's; the time would come when they would not eradicate so easily. She raked out the rats with her big comb and restored her hair to shady respectability with a stiff brush and then a soft one. Her blow dryer would be more efficient, but she didn't want to spend time washing her hair. After some hesitation over her cosmetics, she opted in favor of a light foundation, pale lip gloss, and a baby fingernail's worth of mascara, no eye shadow. She wasn't looking to seduce anyone.

Not that Walker was in any way unworthy. The kind eyes in the mature face, drawn and tired but with an engaging bump in the nose and a wide mouth that fell into a grin without apparent effort, were reassuring, and he had a solid build; but he lived in Peter's world, the one most people only heard about when they watched the news, with detachment and a kind of shuddery wonder, like at the reptile house in the zoo. She might not be able to avoid re-entering that cage, but she wouldn't do it voluntarily.

But she craved human contact. She changed into a winter walking suit and flats and went out to knock on Walker's door.

"Enter, Ziegler."

He was behind his desk, chewing, with a brown beer bottle in front of him and four more in a cardboard carton next to a grease-stained paper sack. The smell of cooked meat, sweet sauce, and sharp hops started the juices going in her stomach.

"Laurie, please," she said. "Ziegler's starting to sound like a lion tamer. Is there any more where that came from?"

He shoved the sack her direction. "Reuben okay? I had another choice, but unexpected company dropped in."

"Are you kidding? Sauerkraut was my first solid food. German farming stock, remember?"

"Thanks. I bet myself you couldn't go five minutes without reminiscing about the good old days in the south forty, plucking cows and milking chickens."

"What was the bet?"

"Another beer." He set aside his half-eaten sandwich, drew two bottles out of the carton with one hand, the way men did, and hoisted his eyebrows. She nodded, seating herself and reaching for the sack. She watched him remove the metal caps with an opener that looked like some kind of weapon. She was looking into the reptile house again.

She ate sitting forward on the chair, her ankles crossed and the coarse brown napkin spread on her lap, holding the sandwich with both hands and laying it on the napkin in its wrapper when she drank. The beer was strong, almost like bitter ale. It paired with the corned beef and kraut like good red wine with prime rib.

"Who was the visitor?"

"Renaissance man. He goes by Stan Kopernick and chews glass at parties." He picked up his sandwich.

"From that I'd guess he's either a crook or a cop."

"Could be both. After cars and empty lots, it's Detroit's chief export. On the other hand he could be straight as a plumb. It doesn't make any difference, because you can be a bad cop and a good detective."

"Is he looking for Peter?"

"Right now he's looking for you."

She stopped eating. "Am I wanted?"

"Billy the Kid was wanted. You're sought in connection."

"In connection with . . . ?"

"Murder, what else?"

She laid down the Reuben, as carefully as placing a bracelet in its case. She swallowed the lump blocking her throat. "Leroy?"

"Not yours. One of your husband's. That's the prevailing theory. We've got a new trade agreement with Canada: The person of interest in the killing of a man named Lennert in return for a case of Moosehead and four dozen Tim Horton's donuts."

"I don't know anyone named Lennert."

"Neither did Macklin, probably, apart from what he learned from doing his homework. The M.O. matched his as well as it matched a couple of dozen others, but apparently he's the one with the quickest access to the border."

"Why couldn't it be a Canadian?"

"Don't say that where they can hear you. There aren't any hit men in Canada. They have to smuggle them in like cartons of Marlboro."

"That's ridiculous."

"You won't get any argument from me. They've got even more wide-open spaces than we do. Up there you can't reach all your enemies with a left jab. You need firepower, and someone who knows how to direct it, and why can't he be somebody who says 'aboot' instead of 'about'? But just now Uncle Sam wants to keep all the friends he's got. So Peter Macklin squiffed Guy Lennert and his ex-wife-in-waiting shinnied down a drainpipe soon after, so she must know something. That's how attorneys general think, everything fitting tight with a snap, like Legos. Stonesmith isn't buying it and neither is Kopernick; but until the president appoints one of them to head up the Justice Department, they've got their marching orders. Kopernick gave me twenty-four hours to hand you over." He glanced up at the wall clock. "Minus fifteen minutes now. You needed the sleep."

"Are you going to do it?"

He finished eating and sat back cradling his second beer in both hands. "Not if I can wrap up Roger on that same schedule. He learned the business at his old man's knee, by observation if not by tutoring. A good federal prosecutor — and we have one here, the same woman who sent up a mayor for twenty and change — can rig him for it, based on similarity of method. Enough anyway to give the Canadians cause for extradition."

"But if he's innocent —"

"Of what, this particular murder and guilty of a bunch more, not counting attempted extortion and intent to kill his stepmother, you?"

The phone rang on his desk. He sat forward, put down the bottle, and looked at the caller ID. "Finish your lunch. You don't want to greet your husband with sauerkraut on your breath." He lifted the handset.

Peter wasn't speaking loudly, he never did, but she recognized the voice if not the words. She knew it better than her own: not harsh, but not gentle either. It was quiet but electric. It always made her think of a powerful engine at idle.

"It's my business line," Walker said. "That means it's going to be busy from time to time. Yeah, she's here. Even sitting ducks have wings, so we used 'em. If —"

The voice cut across his. Walker sat up straight.

"When?" He breathed, nodded. "Yeah, he'll be coming this way now. Sure I'm armed; we both are. Where are y—"

He hung up. "He was on a cell. Either it dropped him or he dropped me. Roger knows you cleared out of Milford. Macklin passed him driving away from my house in a blue Corvette."

"How much time do we have?"

"None at all." He stood and felt for the short-barreled revolver in the clip holster behind his back. "We're going to your room."

"Why mine?"

"Because it's the one with a fire escape."

■ ■ ■ ■

ME

■ ■ ■ ■

TWENTY-NINE

She didn't give me the trouble I was prepared for; dithering over her personal ef-
fects or messing with her outfit. If I'd
thought about it at all I wouldn't have
wasted the preparation. I'd seen enough to
know better.

She wrapped herself in the heavy coat,
tugged on the beret without monkeying with
the angle, and slid the Luger into the saddle
pocket on the right side. By then I'd raised
the shade and with some elbow grease and
an old-man grunt wrenched the window
loose of ten years of paint and six hours of
snow and ice and threw up the sash. She
slung a long leg over the sill and with the
slight assistance of a hand on the small of
her back stepped onto a fire escape that
hadn't been inspected since an honest man
was in Congress. A woman in a million, a
custom original and not another item off a
conveyor belt. Guys like Macklin had all the

luck, and none of the smarts necessary to capitalize on it.

"Hang on tight," I said, joining her on the landing. The heaps of snow had melted, hanging icicles off the edges as far as the first floor, but the iron rail was clammy and the grid underfoot as slick as soapy glass. Our breath smoked in the thin brittle air. The light ground breeze was stiff at forty feet above the sidewalk; it set the whole assemblage swaying, chafed my skin, and made my eyes water. My fingertips began to lose feeling, and we hadn't descended a step.

Something gonged off metal, throwing sparks that burned the back of my hand where I gripped the rail. The bark of the report came behind it like an afterthought. I went into a crouch, dragging Laurie down with me by the arm, and groped behind my hip for the Chief's Special.

"Keep coming, Walker. You, too, dear stepmom."

I edged an eye around the pipe frame enclosing the landing on three sides. I saw someone I knew and someone I'd never met. The stranger stood in the entrance of the alley that ran behind the building, using the other's shoulder as a gun rest. Dr. Chuck, Detroit's answer to Indiana Jones, was standing with his back strained into a

C, with his narrow trunk thrust forward and a rictus of pain pulling his mouth all the way to the corners of his jaw. His stringy whiskers bristled straight forward from his tilted-back chin and his long black hair spilled over the other man's shoulder behind him. They were about the same age, but the gunman's neat haircut, clean-shaven face, and tailored peacoat assigned them to different worlds. His semi-automatic had a brushed finish and reflected no light.

Chuck's voice was as strained as his position. "I'm sorry, Mr. Walker. I came —" A gust of air shot from his lungs in a gray jet. Roger Macklin — it could only be him; most of my enemies are closer to my generation — had jerked at the arm he'd twisted behind his hostage's back.

"— to bring me one of the prints you got from Barry," I finished. "Does it do him any justice?"

Roger turned the pistol, pressing the muzzle against Chuck's temple. "Do what I said or I'll blow his brains out his ear!"

I couldn't take good aim without making myself a clear target. I tightened my hold on Laurie's arm, making her gasp, and fired at the ground. A piece of asphalt jumped up from the floor of the alley. I fired twice more; anything to bring out the reserves.

Something new inserted itself. Roger crossed his ankles and dipped a knee, as in genuflection. Then he straightened, his gun pressed tight to Chuck's temple. His wrist tensed.

The shot made me jump. The ones you fire yourself seem to make almost no noise at all. The unexpected ones are as loud as Resurrection. I looked at Chuck. He was standing under his own power, no longer a captive. From the corner of my eye I saw Laurie Macklin's profile, arm extended, the wicked shape of the German gun. She'd had a clearer shot than I did.

I couldn't tell where she'd clipped him, or if she'd drawn blood at all and had just taken a piece out of Roger's coat. It was enough to startle him into releasing his grip. Chuck ran for the street, wobbling on his legs and holding his sore left arm with his right hand; ran for maximum yardage, but Roger had dropped him like a bad debt. The pistol rapped again. Laurie shuddered; I felt it clear through the arm I was holding. She sagged against me.

I lowered her to the platform. However badly she was hit, she was better off there. I rose from my crouch and squeezed the trigger, aiming for the thickest part of Roger's body.

The report echoed — I thought. Anyway I heard two shots.

The young killer took his time falling. He hung there for the season, trying to bend over backward with both arms spread-eagled and the square pistol hanging limp as a sock from his right hand, then his knees twisted and he twirled down to the pavement like a rope falling into a loose coil. His body humped once, then flattened exactly parallel with the ground.

It wasn't until he'd fallen out of my line of sight that I saw Detective Stan Kopernick standing on the sidewalk, big as thunder with his camel's-hair coat spread wide and both hands wrapped around a black Army .45, a horse pistol that was entirely in proportion with the rest of him. On the other side of the street, a maroon SUV stood at the curb, its tailpipe leaking gray smoke thick as cream. I couldn't make out the driver's face, even though it was turned this way, and the vehicle was new to me, but I had a strong hunch who was driving.

She'd taken a slug in the thigh. The surgeons at Detroit Receiving, our go-to place for gunshot wounds, stabbings, and generic bloodshed of all kinds, said one centimeter to the left and it would have nicked the femoral artery and she'd have died on the fire escape before I could finish dialing 911. As it was they held her a week and prescribed six months of physical therapy.

She was sitting up in a vinyl recliner when I came to visit, in a thin cotton flower-print gown with a sponge-rubber blanket spread over her knees. She wore no makeup, but her face looked fresh and her hair was arranged simply but neatly.

"I guess my bathing-suit days are over," she said.

"Paint over it, or get a tattoo. It could be worse. I've got the same hole in the same place, and that was a lot more serious."

She smiled. "What is it about having a procedure that makes everyone want to compare it to theirs?"

I gave her a stuffed giraffe from the gift shop. "I wanted something more aggressive, but they were out of tigers. Flowers are for funerals. I figured you'd had your fill of both."

She wrapped her arms around the giraffe and hugged it to her chest. "So who killed Roger, you or Kopernick?" *Not me,* her face seemed to plead.

"It was almost a dead heat. The M.E. dug a thirty-eight out of his liver and a forty-five from the pericardial sac surrounding his heart. Either way he was dead, but the bigger slug won the race. That makes eight for him."

"Still. You killed him if he didn't."

"You could put it that way, yes."

"I guess you get used to it."

"Sure. After ten years it doesn't wake you up more than six times a night."

Her face had grown less tight when I'd tagged the cop for Roger's death, but her eyes were opaque. I read what was behind that, and was grateful for it. I hadn't known what to do with the rest of the information. "They found something else. His heart was already damaged, from some old illness. You remember he staggered. Any way you look at it he was dead where he stood.

"Your shot split a button on his coat," I added. "You made Annie Oakley look like Mr. Magoo."

The line softened a little, no more. I'd have to show her the button to convince her, and then she'd suspect I faked it.

"How'd Kopernick get there so fast?" she asked. "He couldn't have heard the shots all the way from downtown and gotten there in that time."

"Oh, that. He sent you a souvenir. I'm playing Santa Claus today. It's not as pleasant to hold as a stuffed toy." I slid a stiff fold of paper from my inside breast pocket, snapped it open, and laid it in her lap.

She picked it up and looked at the Biblical terminology spelled out in Tudor script. "The only Latin I know is pig."

"It's a warrant authorizing Kopernick to search the tailor's shop in regard to a person of interest in a homicide investigation: You. I'd consider changing my brand of perfume. You left a trail all the way from your house in Southfield. Barry Stackpole warned me about the cranial capacity of Neanderthal Man. He didn't say he had the nose of a bloodhound. Anyway he was on his way to serve it when the fireworks started."

"Am I under arrest? Is there a police guard outside my door?"

"He gave it to me as a keepsake. Canada's satisfied Roger killed Lennert: He operated the same as his father, and the State Department's happy no one has to make travel arrangements for him. I doubt Kopernick bought it, but he's got enough on his plate here at home: seven drive-by shootings just this past weekend, a holiday season best. The way he sees it, your ex-husband-elect will wade through mud one time too many and get himself stuck."

"Someone paid to have Lennert killed."

"Remote-control killers are slippery as

hell. In all the time they've been in business, the law's nabbed only two, and that was seventy years apart. With the only official witness chilling in the Wayne County Morgue, the record stands. It'd be awkward to bring forth another witness under the circumstances. Imagine the embarrassment if Macklin were to show up and turn state's evidence."

"So I can go home?"

"I don't see why not, when the docs say it's okay. I'll close out my room in Milford and tell Ralph the Realtor to expect a call from you. I can pack the things you left in my building and send them on."

"You can, but you won't. A girl has to have some secrets."

I moved a shoulder. I wanted out of there. The place had that nothing smell of a modern hospital: no alcohol or carbolic or sour effluvia of the human condition. When the odor alarm sounded, an army of orderlies and candy-stripers charged through with spray bottles, wet-vacs, and kitty litter, with an ionizer chaser. It wasn't of this earth.

"How's Rosecranz?" she asked.

"Swell. He's just glad we didn't shoot up his foyer." I watched her. "He been in?"

She knew I wasn't talking about Rosecranz. She shook her head.

"I wouldn't blame him," I said. "For that. There's a whole shift at Thirteen Hundred that does nothing all day but review surveillance tapes from Receiving. Every inch of footage Macklin shows up on is an inch closer to the house of doors. Every time they see him they get madder and madder. Someday mad enough to hang something on him under the heading One Size Fits All."

"He stands for everything you hate. Why did you take the job? I don't believe for a minute you were afraid he'd kill you if you refused."

"Don't be too sure of that. At my age you've gotten used to breathing."

"You did it for me. To protect me. Why else would you leave a place where you were safe and go out on the hunt for the man who wanted me dead?"

"Safe." I laughed. "What's that?"

Outside the window, snow sifted down fine as flour. They were predicting a white Christmas for the first time in years. I buttoned my coat and turned toward the door.

"Do you think we should have hooked up?" she said. "You and me?"

"You and *I*," I corrected. "Don't talk like a hick. And no. Apart from the fact that you

314

weren't born when I hung out my shingle — with all that entails — sooner or later we'd have fallen out over my career choice, or my working hours, or your clumsy grammar. Find yourself a farm boy with an inheritance, preferably one whose parents are terminal. Grow corn instead of corpses. When you see a hired killer or a private cop — you can spot them by now, I'm sure — cross the street. I'll put that on a sampler and send it to you for a wedding present."

THIRTY

It was coming on half-past eleven on a Tuesday morning, too late for breakfast and too early to drink. So I bought a hip-pocket bottle of Bushmills from a drugstore and put in at a greaseburger palace to fill the vacuum the hospital had left in my nasal passages. It was one of those places where they took your name and when your order was ready and if the traffic wasn't heavy they brought it to your table. I'd drawn coffee from the machine and was stirring in a slug of Irish when a kid came by with my basket of cholesterol. He wore a clip-on necktie with the ends tucked under his apron. That made him the boss.

"You can't drink that here, mister. Not in the open. We don't have a license."

I pointed my chin at the front window. "What's that across the street?"

"An empty building."

"Look again."

"Okay, a blind pig."

"Right. It doesn't open up until the legitimate joints close; and then, boy, it's open wide. Which one do you think the cops will bust first at election time?"

He let the basket drop six inches and went back behind the counter. That was his knockout blow.

I ate without tasting and drank without raising so much as a buzz. It felt like I'd been neutered in some way. I bussed my table, flipped a mental coin between office and home and drove to the office.

This time there were a couple of letters among the junk under the slot. I carried them to the desk and was slitting one of the envelopes when the door to the waiting room opened and closed with a hiss of air leaking from the pneumatic tube. I'd forgotten to switch on the buzzer. I told the shadow on the other side of the opaque glass to come in.

I didn't recognize him at first. He'd scraped the thistle off his chin, caught his hair into a ponytail, and changed from his Dumpster-diver uniform into a clean WSU sweatshirt and a pair of jeans without a rip in them. No overcoat; millennials won't have 'em.

"Not enough for the orals," I said. "Not

quite. You need a jacket with patches on the elbows and a bulldog pipe."

Dr. Chuck's laugh was shaky. He was still going through the aftershock. "Even the dean dresses this way. You're behind the times, Mr. Walker."

"I wouldn't be surprised. The rest of the time I'm behind the eight-ball."

His brow puckered. What I'd said meant as much to him as cuneiform; but he let it slide.

"You might as well know I finish what I start, even if it's too late." He took a four-by-six manila envelope folded up the middle from a back pocket and laid it on the desk.

I put the knife back to work and pulled out a sheet printed on glossy computer photo stock. Roger Macklin's gray-blue eyes looked dead in the blowup from a passport shot. In person they'd danced with psychopathic light. I put it down, swiveled, opened the safe, and took a small brick of cash out of the strong box.

"No, no! You don't owe me a thing. It was a misdeal."

I finished counting, put back some of the bills, and pushed the rest his way. "You came through, you and your fellow explorers. If he'd come at our flanks instead of launching a frontal assault, I might not have known who he was until it was too late. At the very least you earned combat pay. Sorry I dragged you into it."

"I'm not. It made me a hero with my friends, and gave me an end for my thesis. Next time you'll see me I'll be wearing that jacket and smoking that pipe."

"Just don't jump into any basements without looking first." I jerked my chin at the stack of cash. He lifted his shoulders, twisted his head this way and that on his neck, picked it up, and folded it into the pocket he'd taken the envelope from.

"You've got my number for next time," he said.

I grinned at him. If I told him I'd thrown it away he'd just give it to me again.

I read both letters twice and didn't retain a line; I had only the vaguest picture of the acquaintances who'd sent them. I poked them back into their envelopes, locked up the rest of Macklin's retainer, and closed up.

My wipers carved wedges in the snowfall and went back each time for a fresh load. Most of the cars I met had their lights on, some not. There's a rumor going around town that using them speeds up the process of depreciation. I gave them plenty of distance. I was in no hurry. I was just going home to an empty space.

The house was getting shabby. It had taken a few days and nights under another roof to see that. I'd thought it was comfortably lived-in, no showplace but good for a friendly game of bridge, if I played and if I had three friends. I should hire a decorator, preferably one who pranced a little and knew sixteen shades of white by their first names. I put that at the top of the list after the phone bill and an oil change and my dead molar. And making it to Easter with the lights on.

For what it was, that house, it was me: some books, old snapshots in drawers, an heirloom clock, high school junk, a college diploma, my army discharge, and a certificate of marriage that had expired ahead of the Soviet Union. Not much; just the sum total of me.

So I didn't welcome the addition of an uninvited party to my living room.

It was still snowing briskly and the sun had retired behind a ceiling as dark as a killer's heart. The room was dim, but I spotted a shadow in my one-and-only easy chair that didn't belong there when someone wasn't sitting in it. I reached behind my back, in the movement remembering I wasn't carrying now. I seldom need to shoot my way into my own house.

Clothing rustled. The floor lamp next to the chair came on. Peter Macklin lowered his hand to his lap next to its mate. There was no weapon in either one. He wore the leather windbreaker, slacks, plain shoes, a little darkened from walking through snow. I'd never seen him wearing anything different.

"I think I owe you something," he said.

"Not a cent. That last installment more than covered the rent on the room in Milford and my rate for the extra couple of days. We're square. I wouldn't know what to do with that hundred grand you offered."

He knew that for a lie, but he didn't call me on it. Even a cold fish like him didn't go around asking to be insulted.

"I see it differently," he said. "You did for me what I didn't want to do, not counting seeing Laurie killed. I'd have done it," he added, "killed my son. But no man should have to live with that. It's worth more than what I hired you for."

"You knew he had a heart condition. You read his medical file."

"I knew it when it was diagnosed. I'd hoped to capitalize on it, but you got there first."

"Next time drive faster."

"I'm not complaining. As a matter of fact that's why I'm here."

"If you owe anyone it's Stanislaus Kopernick, Detective First Grade, Detroit Homicide. The post office says you shouldn't send cash through the mail, but in this case it'd be the smart thing to do. The FBI's watching both of you."

"It wouldn't be the first time I did that. But I don't pay a cop to do my job for me. I saw the autopsy report. Doesn't matter. You went against my wishes; I should kill you for that on principle. I won't. If you hadn't, I'd be either Ivan the Terrible or Henry the Eighth. Maybe both. I wouldn't care for either one."

"She's going to be okay, by the way. The staff at Receiving's had plenty of experience with wound trauma."

"I know, but thanks."

It struck me then his work came with a heavy overhead. Just maintaining the lines of communication ate up much of the capital.

I said, "I didn't do it for you. If I had any say you'd be on your way to Toronto right now in a wagon with a cage in it. I don't like killers. I don't do favors for them. How's that for principle?"

"Black and white, to the end; so that's it?"

"To whatever end."

He was silent. The light shining down carved grottos in the ordinary face. "I can't decide whether you're courageous or stupid. Most of the men in my line would kill you just for saying what you said. You know enough about me to know I don't need a gun to do it."

I ran a hand over my scalp, back to front, against the grain. My hair crackled with static electricity. Suddenly I didn't care what he did. I'd had a bellyload of the underbelly and no belly for more.

"I'm no hero," I said. "I'm no dunce either. What I am is tired. I've been bullied, shot at, called a killer — when I'm just an amateur — had my house and my office broken into and my personal stuff pawed through; but for me that's just another day at work. I wouldn't be surprised if it's in the job description, only nobody ever gave me one. One day I answered an ad on the back of a matchbook and now here I am, square in the middle of a life of romance and adventure. It gets old, and I'm getting old with it. I don't bounce back like I did when I was fifty. When I'm seventy I'll just lie where I land, like a bag of mush." I waved a hand. "Take it as you please, Mr.

Macklin. All part of the service. Just take it and go."

"You came close to scotching the job in Toronto."

That shook me to the floor. It was as near as he'd come to confessing to Guy Lennert. I said nothing. My voice would quaver if I tried. He was a beast of prey. Once they sense fear they react from instinct, without control. They tear out your throat before they know what they're doing.

He said, "I know you don't like the comparison, but we have one thing in common. Neither of us likes to leave a job unfinished."

He stood, without using his hands for leverage. He kept them free for other things.

"We're not square," he said. "Not yet. You trade in information. I'm not going to talk myself into a life sentence, but I can settle your curiosity as to the other."

After he left, I felt hot and thought I'd caught fever. I flung up the window in the living room and stuck out my head, turning my face up to the snow, falling now in soft flakes that slid down my cheeks like chilled tongues and hung on the end of my nose. By the time they trickled down inside my collar they'd become something nasty, something that lived in the clammy cold under a rock.

I left the window open for the clean cold of the air it let in, went into the kitchen and opened the bar. Something lay bound in a white handkerchief next to the bottle of Old Smuggler in the cabinet above the sink. I took it down and unwrapped a shiny revolver with a deep belly and a narrow cardboard box of cartridges. It was a Ruger Blackhawk, the .357 Magnum, good for piercing rhinoceros hides and Wells Fargo trucks. An antiseptic-looking card block-printed in soft pencil read:

Clean. I fired it once, into a seat cushion.

Of course he knew my unlicensed Luger had been confiscated by the police after Laurie Macklin dropped it in the alley. I'd never know who'd told him. I wasn't sure I wanted to.

THIRTY-ONE

The living room in Farmington Hills looked pretty much the same: red candles blushing in green holders, the cardinal painted on a glass lit from inside, the lamp splashing light straight up onto the ceiling. Still no tree. Today she'd tied back the drapes on the big window to show off a neighborhood in monochrome: white drifts, naked black branches, a sky the color of granite. The clouds were pregnant with more snow.

"So it's McBride again," I said.

Karen nodded, smiling over her drink. "I didn't think you'd miss the name on the mailbox. I had it painted over the day after I got the news about Guy. Does that make me hard-hearted?"

"No. That doesn't."

We were seated as before, the sling chair for her, the gray love seat for me, with the glossy coffee table separating us like a black lagoon. It might have been last week all over again, except this time I'd turned down her offer of a drink. I didn't plan to be there long enough to finish it. At that it seemed as if the world had gone all the way around the sun since I'd been there last.

She was wearing another pair of ritzy pajamas, this one the pale yellow of watery lemonade, with a gauzy white scarf coiled loosely around her neck. The scarf showed off her Miami tan, the outfit her toned body. Her auburn-streaked hair spilled to her shoulders and her cheekbones had been designed to support her golden-brown eyes. Our generation doesn't age the way our parents' did. I was the exception. I felt as old as Stonehenge but a hell of a lot less stable.

"No more Mrs. Lennert," I said. "The poor corrupt bastard. The governments in Washington and Ottawa erased him along with the case, and as far as the cops are concerned he never existed in the first place. He went away like frost on glass."

"I am sorry, you know. I loved him once — I suppose. I always liked him. I couldn't hate him even when he left me for a cheap blonde and a suitcase full of Chrysler's cash. As wrong as it was he didn't deserve a bullet from a punk killer."

"Oh, you heard about that."

"It was on the radio this morning. I guess the police were sitting on the details until they were sure." She uncrossed her legs, leaned forward, and set down her glass. "You were there, weren't you? They didn't mention you, but I remembered your office is on Grand River."

"I was there."

"Amos, you really should retire. You've used up all your odds."

"That's old news. I've been free-falling since the day we met. I almost married you, you know."

"I didn't know; but I suspected. Why didn't you?"

"Dumb luck. That was when I used up the last of my odds. In the long, long series of wrong turns I've made, that might have been the one that put me in a head-on collision with myself."

She paled a shade under the tan. She sat with her feet flat on the floor and her hands clasped between her knees. A bitter smile tweaked the corners of her mouth. "That isn't exactly flattering. I'd forgotten how plain-spoken you were. Now that I think about it, that's the reason we broke up."

"On your part, maybe. On mine it was instinct. Not that I'm psychic: It never occurred to me you were the kind to pay someone to kill your husband. I'm not even sure if that's what disappointed me the most. It was the dipsy-doodle. You sent Macklin — Peter, not Roger — after Lennert, then you hired me. If we got there in a tie and I killed Macklin, the only witness to the deal was no longer a threat. If we missed each other, or if he killed me, he'd be free to fetch back the money Lennert stole."

Her laugh was a short bark. "When did all this come to you, in the middle of a drunk?"

"I can't claim credit for all of it. I worked out the part about you throwing one or the other of us under the bus. The part about you hiring Macklin and telling him to bring back the cash if possible — that I got from the horse's mouth."

I shook my head. "It was a smart plan; the kind that outsmarts itself. All I did was get spotted and tagged for a threat. So Macklin did the prudent thing and ducked out as soon as the job was done, leaving the money behind. Only there wasn't any money in the room, or anywhere else anyone looked. Guy probably wired it somewhere, like I said, only you didn't believe me, and memorized the account number. His girl-friend played dumb. It wasn't a stretch."

"All that money sitting where it'll never

be claimed. What a waste." She sat back again with her drink, recrossed her legs, and tapped her nails against the glass. She was in control of the situation now. "What's your evidence? The testimony of a known murderer?"

"It wouldn't be the first time one of them traded his client for a get-out-of-jail card. It's rare; I was telling a woman that just the other day. You wouldn't know her. She's a lady. It's rare, and it won't happen this time either. Even if he were to take the chance, the cops wouldn't accept it. Too much pressure has been brought to bear from too many places to make them reboot the official story at this point."

I stood. I hadn't bothered to unbutton my coat. I hadn't intended to stay even this long.

"No, Karen, I've got nothing. Just a nodding acquaintance with someone who shares my theory about your plans for Macklin, and that's the man himself. He isn't as likely as the authorities to let a sleeping dog lie, because it's bad for business and comes with the risk that the dog might wake up and take another bite at him. He told me himself we have something in common. Now I know we've got more than one. We've both used up all our odds. If he expects to keep playing he'll have to load the dice. Give him my regards when he shows up."

I showed myself out. When I got into my car I saw her through the window, still seated in the same position, turning her glass around and around between her hands. I'd spoiled Christmas for her. What a Grinch.

ABOUT THE AUTHOR

Loren D. Estleman was born in Ann Arbor, Michigan on September 15, 1952. He received a B.A. in English literature and journalism from Eastern Michigan University in 1974. He spent several years as a reporter on the police beat before leaving to write full in 1980. He wrote book reviews for such newspapers as *The New York Times* and *The Washington Post* and contributed articles to such periodicals as *TV Guide*.

He is a writer of mysteries and westerns. His first novel was published in 1976 and since then he has published more than 70 books including the Amos Walker series, *Writing the Popular Novel, Roy and Lillie: A Love Story, The Confessions of Al Capone,* and *The Branch and the Scaffold.* He received four Shamus Awards from the Private Eye Writers of America, five Golden Spur Awards from the Western Writers of America, the Owen Wister Award for lifetime achievement from Western Writers of America, and the Michigan Author's Award in 1997.